PRAISE FOR TURTLES

Applause, applause for Rhonda Rhea and her daughter, Kaley Rhea! *Turtles in the Road* is heart-warming, inspirational and entertaining.

✿ **Babbie Mason, award-winning singer, songwriter, and author**

With so much humor, *Turtles in the Road* unfolds how the best plan, God's plan, might not always be the expected plan. If you have ever stood at a fork in the road and wondered, "Which way do I go?" you will enjoy this fun read. This book is for you!

✿ **Pam Farrel, author of 45 books, including** *7 Simple Skills for Every Woman* **and** *Men are Like Waffles Women are Like Spaghetti*

At last! A funny, clever, totally awesome book I can't bear to put down. And that means a whole heap coming from a book snob like me since the looming stack of novels I've started but never finished threatens daily to avalanche and bury my bedroom. *Turtles in the Road* will not be part of the carnage. With endearingly quirky characters so easy to love, coupled with smart, contemporary dialogue and a winding plot that sucks you right in, I couldn't give this book higher kudos. Rhonda and Kaley Rhea are two generations of WOW writers; I have just one word for them: More!

✿ **Debora M. Coty, award-winning author of over 30 inspirational books, including the bestselling** *Too Blessed to be Stressed* **series**

Turtles in the Road by Rhonda Rhea and Kaley Rhea is more than a delightful, entertaining read—though it is certainly that. But it is also a gently confrontational read, one that leads readers to a place of facing and dealing with their own issues—i.e., anything that gets in the way of a God-first life. So beware! Though you'll find yourself enjoying the ride as you work your way through this engaging story, you will also likely find some turtles of your own along the way!

✿ Kathi Macias (www.kathimacias.com), award-winning writer of more than fifty books. including her Fall 2017 release, *To the Moon and Back*

Turtles in the Road is the perfect read for a lazy, rainy day curled up in your favorite chair. You will root for Piper as she navigates heartbreak, detours, and a new chance at love. Rhonda and Kaley Rhea's clever wit and natural humor shine through in this sweet, heart-warming story.

✿ Kathy Howard, Bible teacher, speaker and author of 7 books including *Lavish Grace*

This mother/daughter team delivers the whole package: suspense, laughter and sweet biblical truths to soothe your searching soul when it comes to finding God is in the midst of the struggle. Haven't laughed this hard in a long time! *Turtles in the Road* is refreshing and enthralling at the same time. Don't miss this read!

✿ Erica Wiggenhorn, Bible teacher and author of *An Unexplainable Life: Recovering the Wonder of the Early Church*

In *Turtles in the Road*, Rhonda and Kaley Rhea somehow manage to do the impossible. Their writing makes you think deeply about your own life, while you are simultaneously entertained and drawn into their story. I fell in love with Piper within the first two pages. She is raw, honest, and my younger self may identify with her a little too much. Plus, she makes me laugh. This funny, sweet, and inspiring book will ensure you never look at turtles quite the same again—especially if they're crossing the road.

❀ **Anita Agers Brooks, inspirational life coach, international speaker, and award-winning author of multiple books, including** *Getting Through What You Can't Get Over*

What does a turtle, God's timing, and truth have in store for Piper Cope? A future she hoped for but never saw coming. *Turtles in the Road* took me on a fantastic journey where disappointment, doubt, humor, and determination collide. Experiencing this intersection of God's perfect timing and impossibility is what we all long for. The Rhea girls are giving us the perfect summer read of hope with humor, for all women waiting on God. It will not disappoint!

❀ **Linda Goldfarb, international speaker, author, certified life coach, founder of Parenting Awesome Kids and CEO of Live Powerfully Now LLC, www.LivePowerfullyNow.org**

Life is full of surprises and rarely goes as planned. In *Turtles in the Road*, Rhonda Rhea and her daughter Kaley Rhea help us discover that many of life's detours and difficulties are divinely designed circumstances that place us on the path to God's perfect plan for our lives. Threaded with wit and humor, *Turtles in the Road* will help you embrace what hurts and what is hard with a fresh sense of purpose and a heart full of hope.

❀ **Stephanie Shott, author, Bible teacher and founder of the MOM Initiative, www.themominitiative.com**

From the opening pages, *Turtles in the Road* draws you in and keeps you engaged as the story unfolds. I couldn't wait to read what happened next! The characters easily depict the mélange of people we all have in our lives, quirky personalities and all. As they unravel their hidden insecurities, you see the message of God's unconditional love and faithfulness woven through humorous and yet real life situations. I found myself laughing and identifying with the main character, Piper, as she tries to figure out her next steps. If you need a little levity in your life, this story will entertain and warm your soul.

✿ **Cynthia Cavanaugh, author of**
Unlocked: 5 Myths Holding Your Influence Captive,
speaker and certified life coach

TURTLES IN THE ROAD

❁

Turtles in the Road

A Novel

Rhonda Rhea and Kaley Rhea

Bold Vision Books
PO Box 2011
Friendswood, Texas

Published in the United States of America
ISBN# 9781946708038
LCCN# 2017-938002

Cover by Amy Allen
Cover Photo by © Postnikov | Dreamstime.com and
© Gerald Deboer | Dreamstime.com

Interior Design by *k*ae Creative Solutions

Bold Vision Books
PO Box 2011
Friendswood, Texas 77549

DEDICATION

To Stan and Nelda Shaw,
whose love story and laugh story
are so delightfully intertwined.

TABLE OF CONTENTS

CHAPTER ONE

Normally a nice long solo drive had a calming effect on Piper. All alone, no interruptions, just her, the Lord, and the open road. She'd done some of her best thinking on long road trips. Some of her best praying. Some of her worst singing.

She found it difficult at the moment, however, to muster any enthusiasm for belting out late-90s pop lyrics.

Piper took a deep breath, let it out slowly. Sitting old-lady close to her steering wheel, she watched rain fall onto her windshield in a weak drizzle, tiny scattered drops from a gloomy sky. Even inside the car, the air felt damp, too hot without the air conditioner but cold and clammy with it. As her only and greatest distraction from being sweaty-chilled or thinking about any symbolic ironies that might exist between her mood and the weather, she had the windshield wipers. Specifically her newly discovered but rapidly growing loathing for their squeak.

She stretched her neck, working out clenched-jaw kinks. Reason told her the wipers were constructed of metal and plastic and rubber. Rapidly fraying nerves insisted they were made of certified organic fingernails and chalkboard.

They just *kept on.*

Squeak-a-squeak. Relentless.

Squeak-a-squeak. Unending.

Squeak-a-squeak. Back and forth. Until the backsides of her eyeballs were sore from intense, eye-twitching glaring. Until her palms were coated gray with steering wheel residue she'd rubbed off while squeezing and wrenching the grip. Until the terrible, rhythmic squeaking sounded like it was trying to form words, most of them curses.

The small raindrops continued to plummet from the sky, only hard enough that she needed her crummy wipers, not so hard that the falling water would drown out that blasted squeaking. And...and...and her radio was broken, and she couldn't pound her head against the steering wheel and drive at the same time, and the stupid pickup going five miles under the speed limit ahead of her was stupid!

Under normal circumstances, the rain might seem lovely and the broken radio an excuse to karaoke her heart out to a wiper-blade beat and the pickup a stalwart traveling companion.

Not. Today.

Piper thunked her head against the headrest. Twice. It didn't even help to take deep breaths because with them came the unmistakable scent of cardboard in the damp air. Cardboard used to smell like adventure to her. Now it smelled like disappointment. She could feel the sharp angles of the moving boxes pushing into her seat from behind, and she squirmed to find a more comfortable way to sit. There wasn't one. Not in a tiny blue Honda Civic jam-packed with all her material possessions. With a heavy, frustrated sigh she focused on becoming a calmer person. A fruitless exercise. Her brain insisted on creating a world of should-have-saids that would remain forever unspoken to the ex-fiancé three hundred miles behind her.

"Mmmbop!" she sang in a loud bid for her normal enthusiasm. Time to quit thinking about him. "Ba duba dop... No." She shook her head. No, the singing wasn't happening. She caught sight of her face in the visor mirror and poked the crease between her hurt-scrunched eyebrows with an index finger. "You do not belong here," she murmured to the crease. "You are getting in the way of my ability to Mmmbop."

Intellectually she knew she would get past the pain. Even as tangible a thing as it seemed now, it wouldn't last forever. The heartbreak would pass eventually. It had no other choice. God promised He's near to the brokenhearted, and she believed that. But it felt impossible in the *right now* to *intellectual* herself out of the hurt that started the day Mark took her hand and said, "I really need to say some things to you."

She'd let him say all his things. By the time he'd finished, Piper's thing-saying abilities had severely malfunctioned. She'd nodded serenely and thought of adorable baby arctic seals so she wouldn't cry while he told her the generals and specifics of, "I'm sorry, P. But I just don't think this is going to work out like we thought."

The baby seal method worked well enough at the time. She'd kept it together. Hadn't made a scene or cried or grabbed him by the shoulders and shouted, "No, you don't understand. What you're saying is wrong," while the life she'd almost had crumbled to dust.

Now, anytime she saw a baby seal video on the internet, she no longer saw white, fluffy balls of heart melt. She saw a man making a Jennifer Love Hewitt sympathy-cry face and daring to hold her hand while he told her in a bunch of fancy, churchy, I-just-graduated-from-seminary words that God told him she just wasn't good enough for him anymore.

Piper's eyes burned, and she blinked. *Whoops. Nope. Don't you do it, eyes.* She'd done the crying thing. Found it unfulfilling. At least after the first…week and a half. Unfulfilling and, frankly, dehydrating. Enough was enough. It shouldn't sting so much now, right? It had been three weeks. What was the proper mourning period for a two-year relationship?

You couldn't've figured out you "feel called in a different direction" before you proposed? Or before I quit my job? Or even before I moved halfway across the country for you?

16

She shook her head. Whiny wasn't her. But betrayal and anger sat heavily atop her lungs. Like she couldn't inhale without all these *feelings*. Anger was not an emotion she knew well. Not one she dealt with on a regular basis. She avoided angry people. But Mark hadn't even friend-zoned her. He'd, like, God-zoned her. What was that? How could that be a real thing?

Piper could handle rejection. Rejection was… well, terrible, but something everyone had to deal with. Mark hadn't done anything illegal. He didn't have to love her. Yes, he'd promised, but they were not married. He was still firmly within the limits of the return policy. So she could handle that. Had before.

But she felt like an idiot. Because she'd been all in. From the moment she and Mark started seriously dating, she'd known she was seriously dating a future pastor. That seemed big, daunting. Still, she'd helped him through seminary, helped him study, helped him write papers. She'd been a good girlfriend.

And the whole time she'd been a good girlfriend, she'd studied up on how to be a good pastor's wife. Owned it. Planned for it. She'd read all the books, done the research, prepared for the role so she wouldn't mess it up. She'd led the youth girls' Bible study on Ruth—Old Testament stuff—and learned how to bake. How to bake one thing, anyway. And she'd tried to learn piano as a bonus. She was bad at it, but she was trying. She had progress charts! She'd prayed all over her relationship, surrendered to her "calling." When he'd proposed, her answer had been an immediate, joyous, well-rehearsed "Yes!"

Then he got called to pastor a church in another state. All good. She'd packed her stuff, rented a dinky little apartment sight unseen, and convinced herself she could live anywhere the short stretch of time before the wedding. Applied for jobs and found a nice secretarial position that seemed like one more affirmation from the Lord that this was her path. Apartment and job waiting, she said her goodbyes, embarrassingly few as were required. Then she'd followed her future husband with hardly a glance behind her.

Stinging rejection took a back seat to a new reality. Piper felt like a fool. Still. From the time she stood there in the back parking lot of a church far away from home, and worked the diamond ring off her finger. They hadn't gotten the ring sized yet. She'd had to wear it with a little plastic sizer. That hadn't mattered at the time, but now it was a sign. How many other signs were there that she'd been too blind or too busy to recognize? She gave him back the ring because that seemed classy. Then she'd accidentally dropped the clear plastic sizer in the parking lot and couldn't find it again to throw it away properly.

She was an idiot. And a litterer. And her world now consisted of windshield wipers that sounded like the loud and dramatic death of all her hopes and dreams. Or maybe like a distressed possum.

The red truck in front of her slowed to barely over forty. Nice. "Guy, would you just go? It's a fifty-five mile zone, buddy!" She pulled closer to the old Chevy's bumper, near enough to read all three fishing-themed bumper stickers. The road was narrow, had no shoulders, and sloped off on either side of its double yellow lines to trees and underbrush and other hazardous forms of nature. Piper wasn't about to pass the guy. Honking at him and shaking her fist seemed less and less out of the question. "Come on, it's not raining that hard." The squeaky windshield wiper squawked the reminder every one and a half seconds.

Why was she in such a hurry? It didn't matter. Here was this guy in this pickup truck being annoying, and she was thrilled with something new on which to focus her growing temper. An opportunity worth jumping at, considering her alternative was dwelling on where she'd been or, heaven forbid, where she was going. *No, thanks.* Much too depressing, that. Temper had to be healthier than depression, right? Or was that actually a step backwards? How were the stages of grief supposed to go again? *Oh, for crying out loud. I'm someone who needs a pamphlet.*

She'd been so sure. She'd been dating a Christian and a pastor, smart and handsome. He'd wanted her. She'd been so sure. A man like that was safe. A man like that wouldn't go back on his word. Or change his mind. Or trade her in.

"All right, that's it, truck guy." Piper laid on the horn. She bounced a bit in her seat at the noise. *Did I just—?* "Yeah," she said slowly. "You hear that?" She honked several more times in short succession. "I got road rage!" Her heart raced. Later she might question how pathetically exhilarating she found it to be impolite. But it didn't matter. She was honking her car horn at a stranger. Like a baller.

"That's right. Road rage. It's acute and incurable! I am an aggressive person!" She beeped at him a few more times. With all the adrenaline of doing something she'd never done before—something she'd no doubt feel like an utter jerk for later. But she'd never see him again, and she wasn't hurting anyone, and this rage vent was happening. "Yeah! Right? I'm super tough! This…This is a thing I feel fine about doing! You don't know me!" She punctuated each of her next words with a honk of the horn. "You. Don't. Know. Meee!"

The driver in front of her did not seem intimidated. If anything, the Chevy slowed further.

"Oh, come on! Are you…?"

Without warning, the truck weaved to the middle of the road.

"Wha—?"

And then she saw it. She didn't even know what it was, but it was large and circular and in the road right in front of her left wheel. Piper slammed the brakes, cranking hard to the right. Poor choice.

Her little Civic skidded off the road and bounced down the embankment over shrubs and loose rocks, careening toward a line of trees. She squeezed the steering wheel while all her other processes froze.

Before Piper could get a good handle on whether or not she was screaming, the airbag exploded in her face.

CHAPTER TWO

❀

"...Anyway, me and her got married pretty much right outta high school. We're like soul mates. Not to be cheesy. Well, sometimes cheesy's good. I don't know why people have a problem with cheesy. Like if someone brings out a lasagna and they're like, 'Hey. It's extra cheesy,' I'm supposed to be like 'What? No. That doesn't even sound appetizing'? No. I'd be like, 'Cheesy? That sounds like the best lasagna ever.' And then I would *thank* them for making me lasagna and for doling out the dollar bills for the extra dairy. Am I right?"

If Piper's face hadn't already been tender and swollen, and she hadn't recently gotten her nose to stop bleeding, she may have considered pulling the door handle and taking her chances diving out of the moving tow truck. But then she'd have to contend with nature again. Not appealing. Especially since shortly after she drove her car into a tree and its wiper stopped squeaking, the skies had finally opened up to pour rain down on her. She'd met her nature quota for the next forever.

"So anyway," the tow truck driver went on. "Soul mates. I mean, it's pretty much…like okay, imagine someone who gets you so deep, like on such a spiritual, mental kind of level, that they can practically read your thoughts. Me and Kariss aren't exactly like that—that would be kind of creepy and put things like in a whole other category—but we're close to that. We're like somewhere between if you could read each other's thoughts and if…say…you just kind of know each other. Heh. Well, hang on. I guess that would about cover the whole spectrum. Okay, let me tell you a story that goes along with what I'm talking about…"

The driver of the old red pickup had pulled over to help her. He'd been kind to her. *Like an absolute monster.* An older guy with a grandpa-gray mustache. He'd called the sheriff's department and given her a rag for her bloody nose and stayed until the patrol car came. Mustache-guy called her *honey.* He'd even ignored her protests and handed over his nice black windbreaker, which swallowed her and made her feel even more small and young and foolish.

She'd honked her horn at him.

She'd smack-talked him when he couldn't hear her.

If he'd had any decency whatsoever, he would've left her to her misery. But instead he'd given her his jacket. *Ugh. I am an ogre.*

22

But she got her comeuppance. After she'd managed to convince the old man, the deputy, and what seemed like every member of emergency personnel in the world that she would not be going to the hospital, they'd called a tow truck. Payback came in the form of a rumbly white tow truck with "Peeper's Automotive" printed across its side. More specifically it came in the form of the blond-haired, freckled, twenty-something man sitting next to her and only occasionally pausing his thousand-word-a-minute life story to ask her probing personal questions. As if her crisis made them best friends.

"And then…" he said, laughing so hard at his own story he could barely talk. "And then…then the guy said…" He cracked up and slapped his hand on the wheel. "He said, 'Sir. We don't allow *pets* here.'" Then he lost it.

Piper tried to summon a smile. The effort made her face hurt. "Ha. Yes," she said over the engine and the laughter. "That is so… Yeah. So how much longer until we're…where we're going?"

His deep dimples probably made him appear to be smiling even when he wasn't. But she couldn't be sure she'd seen him stop smiling yet. "Five minutes. Give or take. I'll drop you at the community center. They'll have coffee and stuff. You can stay there until I get a handle on your ride, if you want. Not sure how long it'll take to fix it. I mean, Honda Civic. The parts are kinda tricky to find and just looking at it preliminarily"—he took great care and what sounded like joy in enunciating each of the thousand syllables of that word—"you really slammed into that tree."

23

She looked straight ahead. "I really did."

"Yeah. Why did you do that?"

Her jaw stiffened, sending a small shock wave across her aching face. "Turtle," she said through her teeth.

"What?"

"I swerved," she said with perfect elocution, "to miss a turtle." Like a chump.

"Oh, yeah. We have a lot of those. So how old are you?" Hardly stopped for breath, this one.

"Twenty-two."

"Mm. I would've guessed slightly older. But that's probably just because of how jacked up your face looks right now. Where you from?"

She wondered how her jacked up face affected the sizzle factor in the brief glare she tossed his way. "A city."

"Knew it." He snapped his fingers. "Married? Kids? Pets? Hamsters?"

"Nnnope." None of those things. Had he said pets and hamsters?

"Oh." There was a pause, and for that split second, Piper thought perhaps the next five minutes would be spent listening only to the roar of the engine. Then, "Well, let me tell you everything I know about the community center. It's interesting because…it's just super interesting, I think. The thing about it is…"

CHAPTER THREE

Three nineteen p.m. Tuesday afternoon. Jay came to a dreary realization. *My entire life can be summed up in a series of fluorescent blue and orange fliers.* He stood in front of the Silas Bend Community Center bulletin board holding two new such fliers ready to be tacked on. A church promo for a rafting trip a couple weekends away and a reminder about this Friday's pick for Family Movie Night. Something with puppets. He remembered Kent said it was stellar.

He looked across all the other fliers that mapped out his schedule for the next month or so and tried to think of something going on in his life that wasn't on this eight foot by four foot cork board. All he could think about was the fact the Easter border was still up. Which led to *Whose turn was it to change the theme this month?* Which led to *Have I talked to them yet?* Which invariably led to *Wait, is May my month?* And all of it ended predictably with *Then again, is the bulletin board theme really all that important anyway?*

Before he could determine his stance on bulletin board maintenance, Maggie had flagged him down about summer basketball practice schedules, there was some sort of conflict going on over by the foosball table with Garrett Sanders acting as instigator yet again, and Sarah Something was on Jay's heels about her mom saying it was okay if she went on the upcoming bike trip.

So. Many. Voices.

Another voice cut in. "Jay! Hey, brother!" That utterly unmistakable voice.

Jay felt his lips tug upward in resignation as he started to turn toward his friend. "Kent—" His breath got man-hugged out of him all at once right in the middle of everything and everyone demanding his attention. Should've seen that coming.

Kent pushed him back to arms' length, as always animated and profoundly over-caffeinated. "Hey, I gotta talk to you real quick, real quick."

"One second. Ach, why are you all wet? Never mind. Hold on." Jay quickly pinned up the fliers with Easter egg thumbtacks. He spun around to fully face Maggie, standing there with a severe case of mom-look. "Maggie, the schedule sheets should be up at the front desk. Take one. Take as many as you want. Garrett!" he called. The teen at the foosball table looked over with typical, over-acted rebellion. "I see you, man. Make good choices." Then to Sarah, "How old are you?"

"Seventeen." Sarah had her hands on her hips, all but mimicking Maggie's disapproving mom-look and clearly ready to argue her case.

"Awesome. How old does it say you have to be to go on this bike ride thing?"

"Eighteen. But—"

"So is it up to your mom then?"

Her expression went flat. "No."

"Okay. Great. So that's solved then, right? Now go be with your friends."

"But—"

"Is what you're about to say a real concern, or is what you're about to say just complaining?"

She pressed her lips together a moment. "Complaining?"

"So...?"

It took a second for her set jaw to work itself into a smile that looked more self-aware than sarcastic, and Jay gave her mental props for her grace. "So...see you later."

"See you." Before he could even turn his full attention to Kent, the guy was already bouncing and doing what Jay referred to as "dude-ing."

"Dude. Dude, dude, dude. Dude."

Jay knew he'd keep going until he got cut off. "What?"

"I'm leaving a girl here while I work on her car. I just picked her up because she's from outta town, and her car is so smashed. I need you or someone you know to take care of her, show her around, maybe get her something dry to wear, do what you do at community places. Commune with her."

"That's a weird way to say it— Holy cow!" He should've kept his voice lowered as she caught his eye. Probably. But wow.

The girl Kent indicated sat down the hall a few yards, slumped half sideways on one of the upholstered benches at the main entrance.

When Jay was ten, his dad rescued a stray, pregnant cat from the rain after it had gotten in a fight with an animal. That cat had been dead-eyed and pathetic. Still, as far as he could recall, it had been in better shape than this girl. Though showing no signs of being pregnant, the young lady was soaked. Pieces of long, dark hair fell limply from her crooked ponytail and stuck to her face. She wore old, light jeans and a huge black jacket that would've fit two or three of her. And her face. She looked like she'd just picked a fight with an animal. A particularly aggressive animal.

"Do I need to call the police?" he asked.

"Nah," Kent said. "She just ran her car off the road, bro."

Jay moved to turn his back to her so she'd be less likely to overhear him ask, "Do I need to call an ambulance?"

"They did already. She refused medical care. Seemed pretty coherent. Not real talky though, I noticed. Anyway, I gotta go. So. Help her." With that, Kent took a box of picked-through stale doughnuts from the coffee station and headed for the front doors.

"Kent..."

Kent waved his free hand like a Jedi. "Help her." With great flourish, he was out the glass double doors into the rain. Kent was a lot of things. He was even a lot of things all at once. Apparently today, helpful was not going to be one of them. *Thanks, buddy. Love you, too.*

Jay came into contact with hundreds of people a week. He should feel less awkward when introducing himself to new ones. *She might have heard me call her a holy cow.* He approached the woman directly with his most professional demeanor. She had to have heard the whole exchange. Her purpling, swollen eyes watched him as he drew closer.

"Hi. Um...Can I get you a cup of coffee?" he said.

Something resembling relief sparked in her eyes. "For coffee, I would sell you my birthright," she said with utter, bone-chilling seriousness.

His professional demeanor caved into a tiny grin. "Take it any certain way?"

"Sugar and cream. And sugar. And hot. And sugar."

Her nose must've been swollen. Her voice sounded nasally as she tried to talk and breathe out of her mouth at the same time.

"You got it."

It took from the time Jay got the coffee to the time he carried it back for her to wrestle her body into a standing position and shoulder a large yellow purse.

He handed her the cup. "One cream. Three sugars. And here." He handed her eight sugar packets. The way she clutched them in her fist, he assumed she wouldn't be above fighting anyone who tried to take them away. He interpreted the move as gratitude. "My name is—"

"Jay Marler." She took a sip of coffee. Took a reveling pause. Her straightforward gaze and flat tone returned. "I already know everything about you. And possibly about everything."

"How—?" Then of course he knew. "Right. You were trapped in a vehicle with Kent."

"Kent Logan Peeper," she said. Like she was reading flashcards. "Blissfully married to Kariss Madeline Peeper. For seven years on the 24th. He loves anniversaries. A lot. He's been your best friend since the time in kindergarten when he said 'Chase me,' and you said 'Okay,' and you played tag. Also he regrets that the two of you don't have a more exciting story of how you met."

This poor, poor woman. "It was a pretty epic game of tag. So he probably also told you about…?" He spread his hands to indicate their surroundings.

She didn't miss a beat. "Silas Bend Community Center. Established in 1989 by your father, Jesse Marler. I don't recall his middle name. But I do know it was your grandmother's maiden name. You are the current owner. Not actually sure your friend knows what it is you do here. But I'm pretty sure he thinks it might be…magic?"

Jay shrugged. "Sounds about right. You kind of pre-empted the introduction bit. I'm Jay Marler. So you are…?"

"Right." She shook his hand. "Piper Cope."

"Excellent. Nice to meet you. Wow. I feel a little safer now in your assumption that you don't have a concussion. I've never known anyone with a concussion to listen that closely for that long to anything Kent was saying." Granted, the same could be said of those without a concussion. "But…you don't want to go to the hospital? It…doesn't seem impossible that your nose might be broken." *Was there a better way to say that to a girl? Still seemed better than holy cow.*

"Thank you. It's not, though. I'll wait for the swelling to go down. It's fine."

He'd heard the "It's fine" before from people obviously in pain. He knew he should be more empathetic, but…it annoyed him every time. *If you're in pain, just admit it, get it taken care of, and move on. Who are you impressing with your pseudo-heroic denial?* "Sure?"

"I'm sure."

"That doesn't seem…unwise?"

31

"While unwise is kind of my M.O. lately, frankly I'm not sure where I am right now, insurance-wise. But I am very aware of where I am money-wise, so unless I start exhibiting symptoms of something worse than rainbow-face, I'm not going in and paying for an x-ray. If there's someplace around here where I could get a fat bag of ice, and maybe the largest adult dose of any over-the-counter pain medication you might have, I will be forever in your debt. Also, is there someplace, anyplace really, I could go where there is less traffic and fewer young children to frighten? Hey there." She waved over Jay's shoulder. "How you doing?"

Jay turned to see a wide-eyed little Sammy Pritchard gasp and hurry on his way.

Ah. So at least she wasn't acting tough for the sake of pride or attention. Jay scratched the back of his head. "Okay. Pretty sure we can accommodate you. So Kent's taking care of your car. He has your cell number to call when he's done, or—?"

"Yeah."

"Cool. I am going to go talk to my friend Mary, see if she can help. She's amazing." Jay had worked with a lot of volunteer mothers. But Mary was hands down the volunteer motherest. She'd think of ten thousand tiny, subtle, hospitable ways to make this girl more comfortable than Jay ever could. "We'll get you set up with something to wear and ice and that whole deal. We've got a little book nook on the other side of the building with some couches. It's usually quieter there. Does that sound all right?"

"Sounds perfect. Thank you."

"Sweet. All right. You can have a seat here if you want to rest while you wait for Mary."

"I think," she said slowly, looking at the bench with what appeared to be quiet longing, "that I'm going to not sit down until I am somewhere I won't have to get back up for awhile."

Oh, there it was. There was that empathy. Yeah, he felt it now. He wince-smiled at her. "Got it. Just be a sec. After I point Mary your way, I've gotta run. But if you need anything else, anybody with one of these"—he tapped his blue and orange lanyard that held his SBCC I.D.—"would be glad to help you out."

She nodded and looked right at him. Her eyes held all the hallmarks of someone who was exhausted and slightly embarrassed and maybe beyond caring about things like being embarrassed. A stranger in a strange place who'd had a day. "Thank you."

His smile still felt a little like a grimace. All he could think of was that poor, half-drowned cat. They'd named her Swampy. They never saw her again after she ran off somewhere to hide and have her kittens. "Welcome to Silas Bend?"

"I like the…tile choice."

At least she put forth an effort of positivity. Good for her.

"You know. Flooring."

Jay brightened and looked admiringly down at the light and dark gray checkerboard floor tiles. Classy and modern and not blue and orange. "I picked those out last year."

"I know," she said, sounding resigned.

"Kent." He nodded. "Right. I'm so sorry."

She gave a half-realized, puffy-faced expression that was probably as close to a smile as she could manage. He left her there and found Mary in the gym working on a banner for the basketball league. She had her hair pulled back with one of those fluffy hair tie things from the 80s, and her sweatshirt had paint on it from a thousand other banners. At forty-eight with nine kids between eighteen and two, she had a well-earned reputation as a superhero.

After hearing about the young lady's plight, Mary left her various supplies where they were on the gym floor and threatened some kids—half of whom belonged to her—to keep their basketballs away from them. Then she blew out of there like a loud, sweet, well-intentioned mom tornado.

Jay could only shake his head and move on to figuring out the activities for the fourth day of that year's day camp, renting a bounce house for the block party at the end of summer, and cold-calling parents for more volunteers. In any case, much to her unsuspecting benefit, Human Girl Swampy's day was about to get a lot more Mary.

He turned and almost tripped over a staring Sammy Pritchard licking a dripping ice cream cone. Jay stared back. "Aren't you lactose intolerant?" he asked.

The kid kept his eyes locked on Jay as he raised a five-year-old shoulder and ate faster.

Jay sighed. "Where is your mother?"

CHAPTER FOUR

Jay knew there was a room somewhere in the two-story Silas Bend Community Center that had a desk and an ergonomically designed chair and his name on the door. But for all the time he actually spent in that room—rumored to be on the second floor near the mezzanine overlooking the gym—it was widely thought to be a myth. Far more often he was running around the complex, speaking with people, fetching supplies, talking on his cell, making copies, hosting meetings in the main office, fielding complaints, overseeing events and the scheduling of those events, and playing the mediator in the midst of some drama or other. This evening he had to find his way to that fabled room and spend serious time sorting through his files, trying to think of someone who could replace Cam Brauner.

Cam was a nice guy, great guy. Solid. Twenty-three years old, fresh out of college. High energy worker.

Jay even understood where the man was coming from. But Jay also couldn't help being frustrated. He'd told Cam from the beginning that there would be a lot of hours, that this wouldn't be the highest paying gig in the world, that working with people, especially kids—especially kids' parents—took some getting used to. That there would be an adjustment period and a learning curve. Sacrifices would be required. And he remembered Cam sitting there in Jay's office—might've been the last time Jay had been in his office—nodding and promising he could do the job and that he was pumped about it.

That was two months ago. Eight weeks. Eight weeks Jay had trained the guy, helped him out, worked closely with him.

Cam approached him about a minute after a second grader threw up next to the upstairs bathroom. Cam stood in front of Jay, the picture of contrition. And Cam told him regretfully a lot of reasonable things that added up to "Peace out, man."

The guy mentioned the low pay. He mentioned the long hours. He mentioned the difficult people.

All great points. Too bad no one told you about that stuff going in.

All Jay could do was nod. He remembered saying, "Well, thanks for letting me know." He remembered not being very thankful. Mostly he remembered having to blow off the conversation he should've had with Cam because there was second-grader vomit all over the hallway and he had to go find a mop.

Now he was losing his right hand man. Cam's whole job was taking what he could off Jay's shoulders. Now he was just out. People came and went—that was the nature of this kind of work. But Jay hadn't seen this one coming. And now with summer stuff going on… The muscles in Jay's neck and across his shoulders tightened as to-do lists turned to how-in-the-worlds turned to tension. He didn't like being the guy who was wound so tight. He was supposed to be the easy-going one. The guy who shrugged things off. It was becoming increasingly difficult to shrug.

Lord, he prayed as he climbed the stairs to the sound of the church associational volleyball league echoing from the gym. His praying tone sounded not entirely unlike Sarah's from earlier. All the whiny petulance of a seventeen-year-old girl who didn't know why she wasn't allowed to go on the bike trip.

The phone going off in his pocket gracelessly interrupted him. The ring tone was loud, and the ring tone was Bieber. That could only be one person.

"Kent, when do you keep changing your ring tone in my phone?" He only asked when. He'd given up asking why ages ago.

"Hey, man," Kent said happily. Ignored the question completely. "Hey, I'm about to leave the shop for the night. Is Piper still there?"

"Who?"

"The girl with the car and the face?"

Oh, right. He'd forgotten all about her. He rubbed his eyes with his free hand. "Right. Oh, right. The ah…" he snapped his fingers, "Swampy."

Kent chortled. "The what?"

"What? No. Nothing." He shook his head. "I'm tired. What is…? Sorry, why are you calling me again?"

"I've been trying to get her on her cell, and she's not answering. She's still there, right?"

"As far as I know."

"Cool. Well, her car's not done. And it's not gonna get done tonight. Obvi. Kariss is here with me, and she's got her SUV with her. I'm gonna go ahead and close up. She said she'd give Piper a ride to Shawley Bea's or wherever in town. 'Cause she's the awesomest wife in the world, and I love her! Anyway, can you find Piper and tell her for me? Kariss'll be there in like ten or so. She'll just pull her ride up to the front. Like a sexy chauffeur."

"Is Kariss standing next to you?"

"No. Why?"

"No reason. Anyway, yeah. Yeah, I'll find…" Jay faltered. He'd just had it.

"Piper," Kent supplied.

"Piper." *Why couldn't he remember that?* His brain was still stuck on Swampy. "And I'll let her know."

"Thanks, bro."

Jay's phone went back in his pocket, and his body turned to go back down the stairs. He made a mental

39

note to change Kent's ring tone back, but that seemed likely to wind up buried under a pile of other mental notes.

Now, where did we leave her? The book nook. He adjusted his course and set his feet on autopilot. He knew the building backwards and forward, upside down, sideways, and inside out. Navigating the halls no longer took any conscious brain activity.

Lord, Cam's last day is Friday, he picked back up on his prayer. *Well, You know that. Please help me figure out what to do. This is kind of left field stuff for me right now. And I know it probably shouldn't be. I just...I don't have time.*

He thought guiltily that lately his prayer life had consisted of handing God a to-do list. To-do lists had become a ridiculously large percentage of what Jay did every day. Delegating stuff. Is that why it was all too easy to pull that whole list-thing on God? He let out a quiet breath.

Sorry. I'm not the boss. I get that. You are the Boss. And not to tack more on, but please help me have a better attitude. Help me not to get lost in here. In the shuffle. In all the stuff. More and more it's like I'm drowning in it. I love You. You are so good. But I feel like I've got this serious...joy depletion going on right now. And I don't like it. Fill me up again, Father, I'm begging You. Kind of running on empty at the moment. Honestly.

Like many of his prayers of late, he wasn't granted an immediate sense of warmth and confidence. He still felt uncertain and unbalanced.

He arrived at their library nook and once again put his prayer on hold. The nook was no more than a little alcove off the back hallway with shelves for kids' books, a few old movies, and some activity resources.

But there were also a couple of cheap, orange vinyl couches set up on either side for reading or relaxing. On one of them, he found a scene that brought him up short.

That woman was passed out.

She slept sitting upright, held in place by several large, unmatched cushions Mary must've swiped from somewhere. The girl wore a plain, dry, black hoodie and gray sweatpants, barefoot with her soaked sneakers and socks drying by her feet near her purse. She had her head tipped back, mouth wide open to accommodate loud, nose-free breathing, a line of drool trailing out the left corner. Her hair was dry now and frizzing out of its ponytail thing. And it might've been the light, but the bruises on her face looked darker now, though maybe not quite as swollen. An icepack sat melting next to her along with an empty Styrofoam coffee cup, a series of torn open sugar packets, a travel bottle of Tylenol, and a half-eaten chocolate pudding cup.

Jay stood there for a minute. "You," he said, "are having a worse day than me."

Her face twitched, and she winced in her sleep.

Jay decided he better go ahead and wake her. Aside from the fact she needed to leave, if she woke up on her own to find him staring at her, she'd think he was a creeper. "Hey. Hello." He moved his hands uncertainly before he realized there was no good way to nudge her. He raised his voice a notch. "Ma'am? Or…Miss? Hey. Wake up."

"Mmm?" she groaned. Her puffy eyes opened into slits, and her head tilted forward. She stared at him blankly.

"Your car's gonna be in the shop overnight. We've got a ride to take you to a bed and breakfast in town. Okay?" For some reason he felt it necessary to whisper.

It took her a long time to process. Then, "What about breakfast?"

He tried not to smile. "Come on." Jay helped her up and watched as she slid her bare feet into her sneakers without untying them so she had to walk on the smashed-down backs of her shoes. She swept everything but the cushions into her oversize yellow bag. He grimaced but didn't say anything. She'd find that pudding cup later.

The trek to the front entrance took longer than it normally would've. Her steps were slow, every movement stiff and somewhat halting. He'd been in fender benders before. Knew the feeling. He told her the news about her car as they walked. She didn't respond. Kariss was outside waiting where Kent had promised she'd be.

Jay pointed out Kariss to the woman and held the door. "Hope tomorrow is less of…what today was for you," he offered as she shuffled out.

"Thank you…"—she stopped and looked at him, slowly pointed a finger at him, and narrowed one eye—"Jay Marler."

42

He couldn't tell if she was pleased with him or pleased that she remembered his name.

He pointed back at her. "Piper Cope." There it was.

Jay waved at Kariss and waited until the two women were on their way before he headed back to his office. He unlocked the door and fought to remember where the light switch was located.

The small wooden desk across from the door was piled with stacks of old promos, fliers and event calendars, coffee mugs he'd been gifted over the years with kind, thoughtful things written on them, and a bowl of some weird-flavored Skittles he'd thought were the original kind when he bought them—but definitely were not—that had been sitting there for a solid year. The office was a windowless room about the size of a prison cell. That wasn't bitterness or grumbling; that was just how big the room happened to be. Couldn't help that. A bookcase ran the length of the wall perpendicular to the desk, filled with heavy books of varying ages, likely very educational and helpful to anyone who had time to read them.

He moved around the desk and sat in his old chair that still looked new. Then he frowned and stood, pulled out his phone, hit Kent's number, and waited until he heard, "What's up?"

"There's a couch in my office now." An avocado green leather thing. Against the wall next to the door, where there used to be two hard plastic chairs. A puffy, comfy-looking, awesome ugly couch. And Jay was almost certain it hadn't been there before.

Kent's voice was incredulous. "No way!"

"Was that you?"

"Yes! It was! Kariss's mom had it in her basement. Kinda smelled like dog food because, you know, she stores all that dog food down there. Like in the big bags. But I stuffed a bunch of dryer sheets down in the cushions, so maybe by now it smells like...hold on." There was a fumbling, and Jay knew his friend had gone in search of his box of dryer sheets. Didn't even occur to Jay to tell his friend he didn't need to know what kind of dryer sheets they were. Wouldn't have mattered if he did. "'Lilac Breeze,'" Kent said. A pause. "Huh. I could've sworn it was 'Tropical Fresh.'"

"Kent, why is there a couch in my office?"

"Because, bro." Simply. As if that was the obvious answer. As if that was any kind of answer at all.

"When did you even do this?"

"Couple weekends ago."

Jay shook his head with a helpless smile. Nobody really did this kind of thing for other people, did they? "You're a complicated man."

"Right? Well, I gotta go pick up the little man from his buddy's. Oh, I gotta tell you a story about what he said the other day! It was so funny. I gotta tell you this story! Ah, wait. I don't have time. I gotta go. I'm gonna tell you later. You won't even have to remind me. It's so...oh, man. So bye, though. Oh, but sorry about whatever happened that's got you trapped in your office on a Tuesday night. Dumb. 'This too, shall pass,' man. Later."

"Thanks, Kent." He set his phone on the desk and, grabbing a stack of files from the half-open file cabinet drawer, he then walked around and sank into the leather cushions. Sure enough, it smelled like springtime and Alpo. With a grin, he turned sideways on the couch, stretching his long body out, head lying on one armrest, feet slung over the other. He let his muscles relax until he all but melted into this odd, very odd, miraculous, unexpected piece of furniture.

In the relative quiet, with only the faint hum of the building and the far-off sneaker-squeak of grown men and women playing noncompetitive volleyball, Jay thanked God for his friend and for dryer sheets and opened the file on his stomach to search through previous volunteers who might be interested in Cam's position.

CHAPTER FIVE

Piper decided Kariss Peeper was her new favorite person. In the world. Polls were closed, ballots were counted. Kariss Peeper won Favorite Person by a landslide. The woman, twenty-five-ish years old, had long straight auburn hair, big green eyes, flawless skin, full mouth. She possessed most of the qualifying factors for being hated by average-looking women everywhere. None of that had anything to do with her new status as Piper's favorite. No. Her winning characteristic was her personality: there was nothing there. Just a beautiful, barren desert of silence and disinterest. After all the noise and chaos that had been her day, it was perfection.

This lady had looked at her with an intensely unreadable expression and shook her hand with the introduction, "Kariss."

To which Piper had simply responded, "Piper. You probably already know that."

Kariss had said, "Yes," turned and slid into the driver's seat of her black SUV, waited for Piper to get situated and properly buckled in, and had driven off. They'd gone by the auto shop so Piper could get a few things out of her car she'd need for her overnight stay. Kariss made no comment.

That had been five minutes ago. Since then, all that existed was quiet. Sweet, blessed quiet. This woman had married that blond guy who, while perfectly friendly, had made Piper tired just being near him, right? She was his wife. Presumably all the time, every day. So Piper had expected questions, small talk, comments about her current condition of looking hideous, awkward smiles, and assorted sympathetic phrases.

Nope. Silence. Peace. Heated seats.

Piper sat with her purse on her lap, looking out the window, watching small town things go by. Main Street shops. A cute elementary school. Houses. Trees and roads. All without commentary.

Her traveling companion sat with hands at ten and two, looking at the road, driving like a majestic, automated driving robot. Piper kept waiting. Because maybe there would be some other shoe that would drop, and Kariss would glance at her, and the chatter would begin. Another five minutes went by. Nothing. Piper's fingers gradually began to tap the armrest.

Okay, so why isn't she talking to me? It was weird, actually. The girl had to have something to say. They were strangers riding together in a vehicle. They ought to be able to find something to talk about. Had Piper offended her in some way? She didn't see how she could've.

"So what do…ah? What do you do?"

Kariss kept her eyes on the road. Her voice was low and even, and her face hardly moved when she talked. "I stay at home with my son. Sometimes I work with my husband if he needs a hand at the shop."

"Oh, cool." Piper nodded slowly. "So Kent is your husband. That's… How is that?"

This time she did glance at Piper. Briefly. "Good."

"Good." Yeah, so that was a dumb question. "Good." She looked around aimlessly. "So thanks for giving me a ride."

"You're welcome."

She's a serial killer. Naturally. And they were driving through the woods now, trees on both sides. Piper sat back against the seat, resigned. *Ah well. Had to happen, I guess.*

The rest of the short ride passed in resumed silence until they pulled up along a picket fence to an adorable, old, two-story house. Green trim on tan with a gabled roof and a fantastic double porch. Simple but sort of precious. A green and yellow sign hanging from a post in the yard read "Shawley Bea's B & B." Piper's traveling companion drove her car into the circle drive and parked in front of the porch.

Piper waited a beat, glancing across the cab, giving her new friend one last chance to be a violent criminal. Kariss only stared at her. *Okay, then. Not a serial killer. Nice.* She searched the implacable gaze one more second. *Not a serial killer maybe.*

Piper opened her door, grabbed her bag, and convinced stiff muscles to hold her up. She remembered the Kent she'd met that afternoon with his endless stories and questions and laughter and expressions. Looked at the statuesque woman before her. "So you're really married to the guy who picked me up earlier," she said, almost a question, because really?

Kariss's gaze went straight through her. "Of course."

"Of course," she repeated. "Right. Well, thanks again for the ride. You could be a serial killer, and you'd still be my favorite person."

A single eyebrow rose. Somehow that felt like an accomplishment. And then Kariss simply said, "Goodbye." Piper threw the door closed, and the SUV pulled away, around the circle drive and onto the road, driving back the way they'd come.

The checking in process consisted of an older woman trying to convince her to call some sort of hotline. Eventually, though, she was allowed to ascend a wooden staircase, enter the room at the end of the hall, blindly drop her bag, and climb painfully into a much-too-tall queen-sized bed.

She took a deep breath and exhaled slowly. It wasn't even dark outside, but weariness descended full force. She should be praying or something. Probably. But for what? She didn't even have a firm grasp on where she was or how she'd gotten there or what tomorrow would look like. She especially didn't know why whoever decorated this room felt the need to set a lacy-dressed baby doll on the antique dresser. Or why the doll needed to stare at her with its soulless, unblinking glass eyes. Piper turned over.

Dear Jesus, she prayed, barely mouthing the words. *Let's talk…tomorrow.*

CHAPTER SIX

Piper hadn't realized she was being optimistic to think finding chocolate pudding smeared all over the inside lining of her purse was the worst thing that could happen to her that morning. At the time, she'd just had a bath. And a shower, honestly, because she'd really felt the need for both. At the time, she'd been tucking into eggs Benedict—a dish she had somehow managed to go her entire life without knowing she loved—as if it was her first meal in a week. At the time, she'd been able to look out the gorgeous French windows of an entirely unselfconsciously-cutesy bed and breakfast to see trees and flower beds and green grass all bathed in morning sunlight. At the time she'd still been a little starry-eyed that the bed in which she'd awakened had a lace-trimmed princess canopy that prompted her to attempt diplomatic relations with the creepy baby doll.

But then, then, she'd realized her cell phone, while providentially avoiding the pudding fiasco, was missing. Then discovering no amount of makeup could hide her twin black eyes.

She'd hitched a ride into town with Calvin and Shawley Hayes, the most adorably-in-love retired couple in the explored universe—with their charming southern accents and their parental concern and their sweet pet names and their offers to pray for her—and discovered that neither Kent Peeper nor his wife had seen her phone.

Kent Logan Peeper, about whom she now knew more trivia than she did about any given celebrity and most of her personal relations, told her that her car was very severely injured. Not that she hadn't known that. But a timetable of "as much as four to six weeks," depending on a myriad of factors from those hard-to-find older parts to insurance, and that was just…maybe she should've seen that coming, but she hadn't even begun to consider…

But that was fine. Well, that was terrible. But that was fine. She could deal with that. She just needed to find her phone. Because it wasn't stolen or lost forever. It was somewhere, and she would find it and make some calls and formulate a plan. She was stuck in a strange town with strangers, low on money, and her car was broken. But that was okay. She could find her phone and make her calls, and she'd get there, and it was all fine.

"Are you…?" Kent stood there with his name stitched on his shop shirt pocket, studying her. "You look distressed. Should I hug you? Normally I would just, you

52

know, go in for the hug. But you are a 'stranger,' and apparently I 'can't just do that' because 'some people aren't comfortable with the hugging' and I might be making myself 'vulnerable to a lawsuit.'"

There were a lot of finger quotes in there.

"I guess that's just the world we live in. But you are my neighbor. Temporarily. So if you are distressed..."

"I'm gonna pass on the hugging. Thank you."

"You got it." He smiled understandingly, and then with lots of warmth and carefulness, he hugged her.

Piper blinked. "Wha...?"

He was very affirming and encouraging when he said, "You just pass it right on, girl," and then he let her go with a pat on the head.

To be fair, she should've been clearer. And she didn't even mean it in a bad way when she asked, "Are you even a person?"

"We're all just people!" Then he bounced back to his office, calling back, "I'll get Jay on my phone and tell him you're coming to look for your phone."

She trekked the three blocks to the community center. Fortunately she'd worn an old pair of low-top sneakers with her jean shorts and the wide-neck, short-sleeved sweatshirt. She didn't exactly look fabulous, but she felt comfortable. And anyway, it probably wasn't possible to appear ultra glam after losing a fight with an airbag.

Everything was still damp from the rain, but the sun was out and rapidly heating everything up. Though her perception might've been influenced by the fact that her temper was also heating up. *Temper > temperature apparently.* Because this was absolutely perfect, the more she thought about it. What do employers love most from new employees?

I'm no expert, but...I'm guessing it's when they call in saying they're stranded in the middle of nowhere because of a freak turtle accident...

She'd have to figure out alternate transportation somehow. And still she'd be late. Perhaps when she finally did arrive, she could find a dog who could eat her paperwork as well. And even better, maybe her boss would be there to spot her a Benjamin or seven to pay for the car she had to hire to get there before Christmas. Hey, maybe her boss would then offer to drive her all the way back to this nowhere town to pick up her car when it was finished.

By the time she made it to the air-conditioned lobby of the community center, Piper was sweating and taking deep breaths, and it wasn't from the relative humidity. Mid-week, mid-morning, and the place seemed to be in full swing, a blur of stranger-faces and activity. Piper retraced her steps from the night before, circumnavigating the gymnasium to the couch she'd napped on and back. Her search yielded no triumph. She did find a crusty, red-white-and-blue-striped retainer sitting in the drain of one of the water fountains. She counted that significant but hardly successful.

On her way back to the front lobby, she cut through the gym. She wound around the outside of the black stripe on the floor to avoid a couple of serious-looking little girls smacking a tennis ball against the wall on one side of the court and six older teens not-seriously playing basketball on the other.

"Hey. Ah…Piper?"

She turned at the unexpected sound of her name, and her cheeks warmed. Wouldn't have thought she'd be able to tell she was blushing with her face this swollen. Maybe no one would notice. She'd been beyond the point of true embarrassment the night before. Apparently that had worked itself out. Jay Marler, witness to her abject humiliation, was walking toward her. His was a face she'd hoped to avoid, at least until she figured out a way to self-induce a nice case of retrograde amnesia. He looked at her with what she could only assume was self-conscious condolence. You poor, awkward, foolish creature. Which she deserved. Totally.

She worked hard to morph her wince into a smile. Achieved it seamlessly. Or not. "Good morning."

"Morning. Kent called. Said you'd be here looking for this." He held her phone toward her. "Mary found it last night and turned it in at the front desk."

Checking the front desk for a lost item. Something adults did. She thought wistfully back to a time she didn't feel like an idiot. "Oh. Yes. That… She is awesome. Thank you. I really appreciate it."

"Yeah, no worries. Hey, your face looks…less… Hm. You… So how you feeling?"

55

"Better. Good. Still look like I had the Winter Soldier do my eye makeup, but there's also never been a better time to convince people I decimate in secret underground MMA competitions, so…you know. Pros and cons."

He hesitated. "You don't actually…?"

Piper stood straighter. "I do not decimate in secret underground MMA competitions. No. But your uncertainty pleases me," she said in her best Robert Downey, Jr. voice. It came out sounding more like RDJ in *Sherlock Holmes* than in *Avengers*, but it fit well enough.

"Oh, good." He "whew"ed his relief at the ceiling. "Well, hey. Glad you got what you came for. You stuck here again today?"

"Yes. But that's okay, I've got a couple…" she tried to wake her phone. Dead. And she didn't have her charger with her because there was no set of circumstances too small to go wrong. "A couple of calls to make," she finished lamely. Would asking to use their phone—on top of her other list of impositions—be a jerk move?

He waited a tick. "You need to use a phone?"

"Yes," she sighed. "Sorry."

Jay flipped his cell out of his pocket and handed it to her.

"Thank you. Oh, you might be interested to know there's a patriotic retainer in the short water fountain out there."

He raised a clenched fist skyward and whisper-shouted, "Darn it, Jonathan." Jay showed her the swipe code to unlock his screen and left, presumably to collect stray dental hardware and rain fire down on some young patriot called Jonathan.

Piper took a deep breath. The first number she dialed was her sister's. It rang until it went to voicemail. She waited for the beep. "Hey, Laurel, it's Piper. Borrowed a phone because my battery's dead. Just calling to let you know I'm going to be a few days late. I'm fine, but I had some car trouble. Getting it taken care of now. I'll call you when I know when I'm going to make it. Bye."

That was done. She dug a business card out of her purse. It was easily readable if a smidge chocolaty on the left side. As the phone rang and she prepared to grovel, she practiced making her voice sound pleasant without being overly friendly. She had a habit of talking high-pitched and cheery when she was on the phone with strangers. Didn't know where that came from.

She waited for the recorded message and typed in the correct extension. It rang a couple more times before a low, female voice picked up. "Hello, this is Susan Decker."

"Yes, this is Piper Cope. We've been in contact about a job in sales. I'm supposed to start tomorrow night?"

"Piper Cope. Hold on just a moment."

Piper held.

"Oh. Ms. Cope, we've been trying to get a hold of you since yesterday. Your position's no longer available."

Hold. The. Phone. "I'm sorry, what?"

"We don't have a place for you in sales. I'm very sorry. But we do have your resume on file and can let you know when another position becomes available."

"Wha-wha…wait. Wait, how… No. That's… I was told I had a job. I was already set to start. Tomorrow night. How does that…? That can't happen." This was only supposed to be about apologizing over and over and telling them she was slime and she was sorry she'd be late getting there. *This wasn't supposed to be about losing her job.*

"I do have a note here." The woman's voice sounded less composed than earlier. "It's not very clear. But it seems a decision was made to make do with the current staff." Was that quaver at the end of her statement the woman's resignation to dealing with an angry phone person?

Piper couldn't be an angry phone person. Her road-and-every-other-kind-of-rage days were over. She couldn't be an anything phone person because of the loud rushing sound in her ears, the weight in her stomach, and the automatic neuron-firing of *This isn't happening.*

"Would you like me to put you in touch with our HR department?"

Piper nearly said *Yes.* Because she had this sorted, and how could they, and it wasn't fair. But then, what was the point? They hadn't really wanted her to begin with. Laurel got her the job. Humiliatingly. A night shift at a call center and sleeping in her sister's home office for an indeterminate amount of time. None of it was what she wanted, and none of it was what was supposed to happen.

She held the phone tightly and breathed slowly and deliberately through her damaged nose.

"Ms. Cope?"

"Maybe I'll call back later," she heard her voice respond mechanically. Piper was largely not present for the rest of the conversation, brief as it was. Wasn't aware whether or not she adeptly exchanged parting pleasantries or whether her voice was too high. All she could think about was that she'd had one thing sort-of going for her. One thing. A promised job. And she'd lost it. Even if it was pathetic and sad, even if it wasn't what she wanted, at least it had been a plan.

"What is this pattern?" she yelled. It was only supposed to be in her head. But it was loud enough to attract the attention of the tennis girls. While they may have only been looking at her because she'd shouted like a crazy person, their stares activated a burning sensation in her eyes. *No. Oh, no. Nope. This is stupid. I'm not going to cry here. I'm not going to cry in front of two little girls. I'm not going to cry period. For the love… Think of the baby seals!*

But no! Baby seals were poison because of him. She felt her mouth and eyebrows pulling themselves into cry face and fought against it. But she was going down. Spiraling downward in a swirling, rushing vortex of Why? Of Mark and "I love you, but…" and six separate Pinterest boards for a wedding she'd never have and moving and Laurel and a job she'd had and lost and didn't want and was too tired to fight for. A broken car and no money. Little girl athletes staring at her and bruises everywhere and a stupid, wicked, black-hearted turtle!

The turtle. "The turtle." She really needed to stop thinking out loud. But there it was, like a beacon drawing her from the sucking whirlpool of catastrophe. A focus that wasn't hurt or helplessness or questioning or failure. She was stuck here because of that turtle. It was all the turtle. That turtle in the middle of the road that sent her straight into a ditch. What kind of diabolical creature did things like that? It could've killed her! There was a reptile on the loose targeting humans, and Piper Cope could not stand here crying like a child over every other part of her life because that thing was a monster, and it needed to be stopped!

She set her jaw, taking a moment to glance around. Neither of the girls was watching her anymore. Those two future Wimbledon champs had gone back to their game. *That's it. I gotta do this for them. For the kids.* She squared her shoulders and started to make her strong, stoic exit from the gym.

"Piper?"

Piper looked back to see Jay, one of the five people in this town who knew her name, jogging up. He had a paper towel-wrapped item in hand that could only have been the wayward retainer.

"Hold up. Are you done with my phone? If not, that's fine, but when you are, if you could run it up to my office upstairs…"

"No, I'm done. Thank you." She handed it back. He'd already gotten four texts since she'd had it in her possession.

"Sure." Something of her warrior's intent must've shown through in her stance or the set of her face because he tilted his head as he looked at her and asked, "Is everything okay?"

"Yes." It was an automatic response. Because no. But she had a mission now, and that was better than where she'd been two minutes ago. "If you'll excuse me, though, I have to go mercilessly slay a turtle."

"Oh." He nodded. Then he scrunched his eyebrows. "Is that like…a metaphor for something?"

She looked him dead in the eye. "No."

CHAPTER SEVEN

Of all the things Jay had been expecting when he came into work that morning... Wait, had he gone home last night? No. Yes? Yeah, he had. In any case, of all the things that went with a typical Wednesday, accompanying a small, aggressive, very determined young woman on a not-too-covert op to assassinate a non-metaphorical turtle had never made the list. And he found himself regretting that. Because this was hilarious.

He glanced over toward his passenger. She stared straight ahead, exuding a deadly amount of gritty, resolute purpose, her seatbelt secured over a youth-sized catcher's chest protector. He nodded at the road and said, "This turtle's going to regret the day he was ever hatched," in his most serious, militant action hero voice.

"Darn. Straight."

Shoot, her action hero voice could've schooled Liam Neeson's.

Jay might've been a tad concerned when he'd come upon this woman fuming about a turtle that was a threat to the children and her country and all of humanity. He'd prepared to calm her down and defuse her wrath and list logical reasons why it was not a good idea for her to stalk a turtle she'd met on a road outside of town. But then her words grew stirring and heroic, and she'd pointed at Jay, concluding with, "Not on my watch."

Against his better judgment, Jay's response had been, "You're going to need weapons."

She'd hastily tied up her hair and agreed.

By the time he'd led her to the storage closet they used for sports equipment and gave his input on proper anti-turtle gear, he'd found out where her crash-site-turned-hunting-ground was. "That's gotta be ten miles out of town. And, not to put too fine a point on it, but... you don't have a car."

"Because of him," she'd nodded.

"So you're planning to walk there."

"Whatever it takes!"

He didn't have time. He didn't have time to do the things he actually needed to do. So he'd rubbed at his eyebrow and tried to figure a good exit strategy. He was good at exit strategies when necessary, and he was very good and practiced at being a responsible person. But then she was trying to choose between a plastic whiffle ball bat and a lacrosse stick to act as the reaper of her bloody revenge, and there was no way he was going to miss this.

Besides, she was a young lady who planned on walking several miles alone with a dead phone battery. Didn't chivalry outrank responsibility? Chivalry insisted he escort the lady. Chivalry insisted he pretend to believe this young lady was going to find and slaughter a specific but possibly make-believe turtle. Which he didn't. Not even for a second. Which really only made it funnier. Because A: She was so serious. And B: He was fairly certain there was no part of this girl that could kill a turtle if she did find one.

So instead of talking himself out of it, he'd hollered at Cam and told him he was taking a break—ignoring the look of disbelief. He left a note at the front desk, and texted Mary for the not unlikely event she'd show up. Yet it still felt a little like he was cutting class. He wasn't sure whether he loved it. But he was sure it was awesome. He did recreation for a living, but good grief, when was the last time he got to get out and play?

He drove until they spotted her tire tracks leading down the embankment. It took awhile to find a place with enough shoulder to pull his car off the road. Minutes later, they were standing in the woods, him protected by his jeans and SBCC t-shirt, and her by soccer shin guards and knee pads and chest protector and a plastic hockey goalie mask she wore on top of her head because she said it hurt her face to have it on. She also wore a pair of fingerless knit gloves she must've had in her purse. All the bruising around her eyes acted as spectacular black camouflage paint. The whole picture was the most committed representation of nonsense he'd ever seen.

Jay waited a beat as a car drove by on the road a few yards behind them. "So what now?"

She motioned with her lacrosse stick. "Fan out."

"Right. I'm gonna need a description of the target."

She squinted at him with borderline condescension. "It's a turtle."

"How will I know whether it's the right one?"

Woman didn't miss a step. "The aura of red, glowing evil that surrounds it."

"Obviously."

"Obviously," she agreed.

"How do you know it wouldn't have, you know, moved on by now?"

"Villains always return to the scene of the crime. Everyone knows that."

Right. That made as much sense as anything else about this mission.

The ground was wet and soft. It took careful maneuvering to avoid the hazardously muddy places. The underbrush was overgrown but not impassable. The noise he heard confirmed his hunting partner (commanding officer?) was hacking away at it with her lacrosse stick. And seemed to be enjoying it.

"Is there a verbal signal we should use when we spot our quarry?" he called over.

"Um. 'Found it'?"

"Seems a little uninspired."

"You want a codeword?"

"Or, you know, I could do like a pigeon sound." He actually did his fairest imitation of a velociraptor.

She paused in her attack of the shrubbery to stare at him with a bewildered expression. "What kinda pigeons you got around here?"

"You've already seen the sort of carnage our turtles have wrought."

Her answering huff might've been laughter, but he couldn't tell for sure. She resumed moving forward while sweeping the area with her weapon.

Jay hopped up on a rock. "What is this method you're using?"

"Pretty sure you're not supposed to talk while hunting," she grunted.

"So this is stealth mode for you. Okay."

"I'm being intimidating. What's the turtle gonna do? Run away?"

"Then why can't I talk?"

"I just thought it was against the rules of hunting. Go ahead and talk. Scare away the demon pigeons—whoap."

Jay didn't see her fall. But it was almost better for that. The sound of too much mismatched sports equipment locked in a struggle with gravity before the inevitable sound of a body hitting the earth with a dull, wet splat. It took him a few seconds to pick his way over, and by the time he did, she was still sprawled on her back. The hockey mask had been knocked forward to half-cover her face, but her mouth was still visible. It was making the straightest-line mouth he'd ever seen on a human face. She said one word. "Mud." It could've been way worse.

Jay covered his mouth. Because there was no chance his human face would hold a straight-mouthed expression. "What have you done?"

"There were thorns. And I tripped," she said. "And then I just kept tripping."

If he held back his laughter any longer, he would bruise his ribs. "Are you…?"

"Nope! No, that's it. That is it." She used the lacrosse stick to pull herself up to her knees. The back of her was brown mud from shoes to hair. She fixed the hockey mask up on her head. He hadn't noticed her eyes were brown, too. And fierce. "Turtle soup on the menu tonight!"

"We have to eat it after we kill it? Because I only signed up to be part of the violent blood feud."

Piper struggled the rest of the way to her feet. "Come on! This way." She tramped off.

"This way. Based on what?"

"Water flows downhill. Turtles like water. Probably. I know how this turtle thinks! He's this way. We find his den. And we smoke him out."

"We smoke him out of the water?"

"We metaphorically smoke him out," she amended. She was slowing down. Breathing hard. The lacrosse stick had become more of a cane than a machete. In her defense, though, it was hot, and she was carrying a lot of extra weight in mud and body armor. They fell into silence as they trail blazed. He'd give it another ten minutes before she got whatever this was out of her system and started the journey back to the car. Fortunately, he thought he still had a slip-n-slide from last summer in his trunk he could use to protect the passenger seat.

Jay's phone buzzed in his pocket a couple times, and he automatically reached for it. But he stopped. For one, his right hand had mud on it from navigating a steep part of ground. For two, when had reaching for his phone become such a conditioned response that his brain hardly registered it anymore?

It can wait. It can wait an hour. It could, right? Usually he was convinced it couldn't. But out in the woods, without the community center walls all around him, it seemed like whatever his phone was buzzing about could wait an hour. Maybe he'd regret it later when he was tired and still had too many things to do. But at the moment…

"Turtle!" The shout came loud and sudden and hardly seemed to believe itself. Piper dropped to sit on her heels on the slope, pointing with her lacrosse stick.

"Turtle! That's a turtle! Holy smokes, there's a giant turtle! Giant turtle right there! Twelve o'clock!"

He followed her gaze. Because surely not. "Are you kidding me?" But there it was. On a fallen log. Looking like it had been waiting for them. Brazen, with its head and all its appendages sticking out of its shell. It was a big sucker, too. At least ten inches in diameter.

"Look!" she hollered at Jay. "Look. That's a real turtle! Do the thing. Do your pigeon shriek!"

He still couldn't quite wrap his head around it. "Did you set this up? Somehow?"

She jumped up, approaching the turtle cautiously. "We weren't supposed to actually find one." Then she shook her head. "I mean…I knew it! We meet again. Beast. You and I have a score to settle."

Jay crossed his arms and grinned. This was a kick in the teeth to anyone who would ever say God had no sense of humor. "This is the one that destroyed your car then?"

"Absolutely," she growled and held the lacrosse stick like a baseball bat.

"Yeah. You'd never forget a face like that." It was a turtle. It looked like every other turtle he'd seen. Dark green shell with bits of orange around the edge, striped face. Turtle.

"Right. Prepare to meet your doom!" She choked up on the stick, tightening her grip in preparation for a vicious, shell-cracking swing. Then she loosened her hands. "You know, I don't like that. 'Prepare to meet your doom.' That's amateur hour. 'Say your prayers'?" she tried. "No. No, I hate that more."

Jay offered his help. "'Hope your turtle life insurance is paid up'?"

"No. What? No, that's not even scary. Sounds like before I revenge-kill him I'm interested in looking over his turtle portfolio."

He tried a scarier voice. "'Say hello to turtle Satan for me.'"

She held up a contradictory index finger. "That doesn't seem theologically sound. And also: What is that? I'm friends with turtle Satan? 'Say hi and tell him it's been too long, and would he and the missus like to come over for tea and biscuits?'"

"Is turtle Satan…British?"

"There is no turtle Satan!"

"Right." He nodded. "All right. How about 'You have failed this…small town'?"

She scowled. He didn't know her well enough to be sure, but he thought maybe she was fighting a smile now, too. "Derivative."

"Well then I don't know what to tell you. I don't see how you can, in good conscience, sacrifice this wild turtle on the altar of your fury without some memorable parting words."

Piper frowned. It might've partially been a pout. But it was mostly a frown. She looked at the turtle for a long time, considering. It was incredibly difficult for Jay not to grin. *I was so right.* This turtle had nothing to fear from the human-shaped mud monster that stood eyeballing it with a far too serious expression. The turtle didn't move. Just held its head up regally, gazing into the distance, looking indifferent and opinionated all at once.

She did surprise Jay by slowly reaching out and stroking the turtle's shell, and that made the thing finally retreat into its armor. She sighed. Her shoulders slumped forward. "Fine," she mumbled.

He took that to mean they'd be heading back to the car.

"Can you hold the net stick?" she asked, holding it out.

He took it from her. "It's for lacrosse. And yeah… What are you doing?" She'd picked the turtle up and held it in both hands out away from her body. He panicked. "Oh gosh. Are you really going to eat it?"

"No," she said, and she seemed angry about it. "I'm going to adopt it and love it and take care of it and its stupid cute, sad little face. Everything is terrible."

Hm. Well. He hadn't expected that.

CHAPTER EIGHT

Piper's arms ached from holding the turtle above her lap, but she was afraid that it would bite her. Or poop or something. Because it was a wild animal, and wild animals did those sorts of things. *Oh, what am I doing? This is not a good idea. What am I doing?*

Apparently she had lost the ability to make good decisions altogether. And she had failed like never before in at least the last two choices she'd made for anxiety vents. *Have I ever made a good decision?* She remembered thinking Mark was a great decision. *Oh, dear. Oh, no. Is this who I am now?* It didn't feel like it. At least before when she'd made a bad decision, she'd done her homework first. Since when was her bad decision making an off-the-cuff thing? And how had her little improvisation led her to this place? Sitting in a more-or-less random guy's car on top of some kind of long, plastic yellow tarp, holding an undomesticated reptile. Could reptiles even be domesticated?

Her mud was beginning to dry into an uncomfortable crust.

"So…what are you going to name it?" Jay asked. His voice sounded tentative.

She had to give him credit. If she'd just met her, she would've thought she was a total psychopath. The peak of a couple of pretty ridiculous stress-vents. The fact he hadn't run screaming made her both appreciate him and question his judgment.

"You are a very good sport," she said.

He grinned. A quick, crooked type affair. "Nah. I was just wooed by the thrill of the hunt. And, I didn't have a lot of faith in your ability to not…die in the woods?" He pulled a series of comically remorseful grimaces and tapped on the steering wheel. "I probably haven't known you long enough to make that kind of joke. I'm sorry. I take it back. I'm going to stick with the 'thrill of the hunt' part of what I said."

She chuckled through her nose and then winced because her nose still felt like she'd been slugged. Oh, he was awkward. Kind, but awkward. She was grateful for his awkwardness, though. It was a comfortable sort of awkward, and it made her feel like less of a total catastrophe. "Well good. It's not like I've given you any cause to doubt my survival skills."

"Nooooo…" he assured her, graciously taking part in her lie. "So. You are okay, right? And that's not… I don't mean that as a leading question."

"What does that mean?"

"You can say you're not okay." He shrugged. "I just know that before you used my phone you were slightly less homicidal than after you used my phone. Even if you are honestly not good at homicide. Turtlecide?"

Her turtle had popped his head and legs out, watching her and kicking all its limbs like a puppy held over a bath. Brave little guy. She couldn't help a swell of affection, even though it was silly. Of course he was brave. He was her turtle. He'd beat her in a game of chicken, and she'd found him in the woods. Because of course, it wasn't possible this was a different turtle. They had a bond.

Okay, so it was a random turtle. But finding him did something to her. Clearly the something was stupid and pathetic, but she'd seen the hard-shelled beast looking back at her and found herself thoroughly incapable of leaving it there. He looked sad. Was she projecting? That would mean she was sad. She thought she was over being sad. That was the whole point of anger, wasn't it?

"Anyway," Jay went on.

Had she been ignoring him?

"I didn't know if you got bad news or what."

"I got slightly bad news," she confirmed. "The job I had lined up fell through. Which is fine. But the reality of the situation is…" She sighed with the weight of the situation. It wasn't even hopeless. If it had been hopeless, maybe there would've been some dignity about it. "I'm going to have to see about borrowing some money from my sister and her husband. Which will probably be fine, honestly, and I'd have to do it anyway. I just," she glared at her turtle, "I hate that. I'm already going to have to crash at their apartment for I-don't-even-know-how-long until I can find somewhere else to live. Somewhere. Now I'm going to owe them more, and I've got no source of income. It's annoying. That's annoying, right?" She booped her turtle on the top of its head, and he pulled it inside his shell. "And now I've got another mouth to feed." She took a cleansing breath. *Was I this dramatic when I was engaged?*

"You talk to her yet? Your sister?"

"Nope. Trying to work out exactly how to approach it. The whole hat-in-hand thing—I've always found it difficult." She was still trying to hang onto some last vestige of pride? Would've thought that would've been demolished with the front end of her vehicle. Or in that mud pit back there. "Not least because I do not look good in hats."

"There is a goalie mask on your head," he pointed out.

Too true. "Well. That was to pull together the outfit."

"So you're essentially jobless and homeless. In addition to carless."

"You're essentially blunt." Piper couldn't even be annoyed.

He cringed an apology. "Not usually. Promise."

"I don't mind blunt. Anyway, I'm not usually… what you've learned about me through the duration of our short time together." The tarp beneath her rustled as she shifted in her seat.

"So usually…?"

"Historically there's been less mud. Yes. Significantly less. And usually I spend more time in prayerful consideration before I take off after smallish creatures in a frenzy of…" Like slaughterousness, except angrier and an actual word. She absently rubbed the underside of the turtle's shell with her thumbs. "What's the word I'm thinking of?"

"Bloodlust?" he offered immediately.

"Perfect." Piper glanced sideways at him. She'd just met him. But couldn't every town use a person who could be casually handsome, frighteningly nonjudgmental, and ready with the word "bloodlust" at a moment's notice? "Thank you."

He nodded at the road. "Who do you pray to when you're considering?" he asked. "Historically?"

Piper pressed her lips together, feeling inexplicably caught out. For a second, there was panic. And it wasn't because she was ashamed of Jesus. It was because she couldn't be sure that this man knew Jesus, and if he didn't then she would at that moment be representing Christ and Christianity in general. And for Pete's sake, what if he thought the church was full of a bunch of weirdos, and she cemented that belief in his mind for the rest of his life? His eternal soul might be on the line here!

Oh, God. Oh, help. Holy Spirit, I know saving souls is your thing, and I have nothing to do with it, and you're more than able to override my stupid bad impression. But please, oh please, help me not be a great big stumbling block for this nice man who's driving me and my turtle around during a workday.

Piper cleared her throat. "Jesus," she answered. Super chill.

"So you're a Christian." He blessedly did not seem to notice her brief bout of alarm.

"Yep. God really changed my life," she said weakly. And it was true; He had, miraculously. But what if Jay thought God had changed her life into this?

"That's awesome." He smiled easily. "Me, too."

"Oh, thank God," she said. Had she been holding her breath? She looked over at his startled face. "I mean literally. Because you know how some people have like a Christian-radar where they can just sort of tell who knows Jesus and who doesn't? 'Discernment' I guess? Well, apparently I don't have that, and I was really scared you might be looking for answers and purpose and all the things that humans do when they haven't met Christ yet, and then your impression of Christians was going to be me like this, and…that would've just been…the worst. For you," she finished lamely and winced. Her hands were too full of turtle for a proper, old-fashioned facepalm. A blessing for sure, because her face was hardly up to it. "Ahhh. So how 'bout that Bible, though? That's good stuff."

"It is." He was laughing at her. But it seemed like he was trying not to. "I'm just over here agreeing with you." With short, face-distorting, close-mouthed chortles.

"You are chortling."

"I'm not. I'm sorry. Don't look at me." He waved her away and then shot her a glance anyway. "I really appreciate your concern. Honestly. I do." The sentiment was a little undone by the chuckling. But Piper reluctantly found the chuckling contagious anyway.

"I was having a crisis," she pointed out, but her tone failed to sound appropriately scolding.

"I realize that. I'm so sorry."

"What if I hadn't been a Christian? You asked a leading question that time for sure. What if I hadn't said I pray to Jesus?"

"I thought you would. I have better radar than you I guess. Praydar?"

"Praydar." Definitely. "But you would've shared Christ with me," she checked.

"I would've. Of course. 'Girl, you need Jesus.' Just like that."

"Good. I do need Jesus."

"Me, too," he said.

The car pulled up to Shawley Bea's. He didn't hesitate before parking and turning it off. "Come on," he said. "There's a hose out back by the garden. If you track mud through her foyer, Shawley will be less likely to overlook the idea of you keeping a turtle in your bathtub. She gave you the room with the…?"

"En suite? Yeah."

"Perfect. You go out back. I'm going to talk to her."

"Why?"

"Because she loves me, and you need a character reference."

Piper was bruised and covered in mud and odd sportswear and holding a large turtle. "Please tell her I'm not super weird." She tried to keep the desperation out of her voice. "And…try to believe it while you're saying it?"

"You got it." Jay got out of the car and then stuck his head back in the open driver's side window to talk to her. "Wait, what's the turtle's name?"

"What?"

"If it has a name, she'll be more likely to see it as a beloved pet."

"He is a beloved pet. His name is…Martin?" It felt wrong the moment she said it.

Jay looked similarly doubtful. "He looks like a Martin?"

"What's wrong with Martin?"

"Nothing. Well, I knew a Martin in sixth grade." He looked even more doubtful.

"Was he mean to you?" *Martin, how could you?*

"No. He just never struck me as a…turtle. It's weird. I don't know. Are we even sure this turtle's a boy?"

"We're about fifty percent sure. I'm not checking." She didn't mean to sound so scandalized.

"I'm not checking. I'm not even sure how…to finish this sentence." Jay looked the most doubtful she'd ever seen.

"Well, if not Martin, then what does this turtle look like?"

"A hubcap. Sort of."

"Come on, I can't call him…" Wait. Oh that was interesting. "Hubcap. Hubcap. Hubby. Hubs. Cap. Cappy Cap. El Capitan. Hubbadubdub. H-Cap. HC."

Jay seemed vaguely frightened. "What's happening?"

"Hubcap. That's it. That's his name. Nice work." She looked at the creature's lazy, reptilian face and wished she could hug or nuzzle him without fearing he would do some damage to her person.

"Hubcap it is." Jay tapped the top of the car like a judge. "I'm going to talk to Shawley."

"Ooh, tell her I can make English matrimonials!" Piper called out the car door.

"You what?"

"It's like an oatmeal cookie bar but with jam in the middle." It seemed, if the furrowed brow and inquisitive frown were any indication, he did not know how to integrate that information into his pitch. Or why he should. "It's not much. But it's what I have to offer. If she lets us stay, I'll make her a batch of baked goods. Oh, and tell her it's only just for the one night. I'm hoping I can get to my sister's by late tomorrow."

He looked at her thoughtfully for a moment before nodding. "Got it."

"And thank you! Every town should have a you."

Jay's thoughtful look bloomed into a surprised smile. He didn't say anything, but he tilted his head in a nod. He jogged up the porch steps, toeing out of his muddy shoes by the welcome mat before popping inside the front door.

Piper cringed. She probably shouldn't have said that. Was that flirting? It wasn't, right? She didn't mean it flirty. She'd had fun and thought he was kind and only wanted to say so. She hadn't had to worry about what might be flirting when she was engaged because of the understanding that she was engaged. Being single was weird. But it didn't matter. She'd only be here another day.

Hubcap caught her attention, busy flicking his feet again. She narrowed her gaze in accusation. "Why are you so cute?" She'd have to do a thorough investigation on the care and maintenance of turtles. "You're an adorable turtle. Are you even a turtle? Or are you a tortoise?" Was there a difference? "There is so much I don't know."

The car door groaned as she pushed it open with her elbow, and she sang along because she knew all the words. As she made her way around the side of the house, she found herself praying half-thoughts and broken phrases. *Don't know what I'm doing* and *Help me not accidentally kill this turtle* and *Money* and *Car* and *I don't think my sister really likes me* and *My fault and Mark's fault* and *Can't and Help?*

She thought it odd, as she walked by the flowerbeds and a pretty mosaic bench and the cutest outdoor table set, that she wasn't even really unhappy. What she felt wasn't unhappiness at all. It wasn't happiness, certainly, but it wasn't the opposite. She felt weary. Her heart felt heavy, heavier than the shell-reinforced creature she held in her hands. There had been too much, too fast, too consecutively, and she was tired.

God, I feel empty. And whiny. And muddy. And... that I'm doing everything wrong. Please, fill me up, Lord. Give me direction. Give me something from Your Word. I'm too exhausted to rest, even to rest in You.

She set Hubcap down in the grass and cranked on the water at the spigot. She pointed the end of the hose at her muddy feet. Maybe she should strip the sports gear off first? Too late. The water surged out of the hose. She forgot all about weariness and rest because this hose apparently was fed directly from an alpine glacier.

CHAPTER NINE

Jay hadn't gotten farther than asking Shawley and Calvin their impression of their newest guest when they heard a high-pitched "Whoop!" from the backyard. They moved their loose circle to the French patio doors and watched Piper struggle to hold still under what looked like an uncomfortable spray of water.

Shawley and Calvin Hayes were polite, classy people. In keeping of his high opinion of them, they both took a step back from the glass to ensure Piper wouldn't see them before dissolving into a fit of laughter.

"Oh, honey," Shawley sniggered, and it wasn't clear who she was calling honey.

Calvin removed his glasses to wipe his eyes. "What's happened now? Is she always so…?" he gestured at her.

"To be fair, this is only her second day here," Jay said. "But yes, so far, she is always so…" he repeated the gesture. Jay related the adventure in turtle hunting. Shawley laughed so hard she could only interrupt to offer him food three times. While he talked, he glanced periodically at Piper. She alternated between braving the water hose and darting away from it to pick up her shockingly active turtle and return him to his original position.

"Well, she seems like a sweet girl. Bless her heart." Shawley wore that expression Jay had seen many times before—on parents watching their little angel hit a foul ball and run to third.

He had a cup of coffee in his hand and couldn't remember when he'd acquired it or from whom. It was delicious. "Oh. Thank you for this," he said to both of them.

They did that quick, amused exchange of a look that had caused him to wonder since he was nine years old if they might be telepathic.

Calvin said, "So you're thinking something. You look a whole lot like you're thinking something." He used to say the same thing when Jay was a teenager and Calvin suspected he liked a girl. This was the first time he was not correct. But Jay couldn't say he wasn't thinking something.

Shawley cut in before he could answer. "He looks a whole lot like he's not getting enough time off. I'm just glad to see you during the week. Anymore it's a quick hey-hello after church on Sunday and then you're off running, looking near to give out." He heard more concern than disapproval in her voice.

"Next you're going to tell me I look too skinny, honey, and am I even eating?" He could do a decent imitation of her faint accent. His Miss Shawley impression was much celebrated and an easy crowd-pleaser at local events.

The dishtowel that hit him in the face wasn't entirely unexpected. It was a popular part of her bit. He should have realized she'd have one within reach. Flying dishtowels were an extension of her person.

"You hush," she blustered through a grin. "You make me sound like an old lady."

Jay tipped his mug to her. It had been too long since he'd been in the Hayes' sitting room drinking coffee and failing to dodge dishtowels. "Not old. Wise. I'm here to inquire after some of that wisdom. I need your godly counsel."

Calvin raised an eyebrow. "I thought you were here to deposit our most recent guest. Or guests, I suppose it is now." Calvin would never care if he had a turtle staying in one of the upstairs bathtubs. If anything, he was probably happy to have a new story to tell.

"Well, I've got an idea. And I wanted to hear, right out of the gate, whether or not you thought it was terrible."

That got their attention. He wasn't even sure if it was worth mentioning. But he'd been praying for a solution to his problem, and here was a person with problems of her own. Maybe this was God divining an opportunity. He checked out the window. Piper had divested herself of battle gear and shoes and sat sprawled on the lawn, soaked and studying a turtle that now wore the hockey mask fixed atop its shell. Even from this distance, it looked creepy. Maybe this was God divining an opportunity to laugh.

❀

"If there was a job available here for the summer, would you be interested?"

Piper squinted up at Jay. He obligingly moved so the sun wasn't directly behind him. It took her a moment more to understand the question he'd just thrown out with no preamble whatsoever. She looked back at Shawley Bea's. "Oh. I don't think they need help here."

"No, I mean here in Silas Bend."

"Yes," she answered. Should have hesitated. Should have at least comprehended the question. "Wait. No. Wait. Doing what?"

"I just lost my right hand man at the community center. It's long days, and you'd be making almost nothing, and it's the most fluid job description in the history of job descriptions. But if I could work out a deal with Calvin and Shawley about you staying here for a lower rate while you're working in town, would you be interested?"

"Yes. Wait." *Ask. More. Questions.* "Are you serious? Why? I'm a mess. And insane. I have a turtle, Jay."

His fingers tapped at the side of his leg. Was that impatience or nervousness? He had zip reason to want her to say yes. Unless he was nervous because he was afraid she would say yes. But she wasn't getting that from him at all.

"I'm in a bind," he said. "And you're in a bind. Plus I think you might really do a good job. You communicate well. You're goal-oriented."

"My goal was to annihilate this animal, and I have adopted it." It was pleasant that they were outdoors because her voice had gotten a few shades too loud.

"So you're a nurturer. And you're high energy. Even right after a car accident. You're really very high energy."

Good heavens. He was arguing her side. "But," she said, "I got your stuff all muddy." She let her gaze trail up to where the equipment now sat in a sopping pile on the patio.

"So I can't give you back your deposit." He shrugged. "Listen, it seems like you're learning how to constructively handle stress—sort of. You're obviously a team player, if your facility to recruit me earlier is any indication. And you don't say bad words when you fall down."

He ticked them off like bullet points on a resume.

"Presuming the background check comes back clean" he said, eyebrows quirked, "that's exactly what I need if I want to survive this summer with my sanity intact." He cleared his throat. "The background check will come back clean, right?"

Piper wanted to rejoin with something cool and clever. Nothing came to her. Before her stood this enigmatic man and his strange words and the unbelievable matter of his offer. She had lost all ability to rejoin. Even joining seemed like a long shot. "I...you...yes. It will."

"Okay. So?"

"You want an answer right now?" She wanted to give an answer right now. But the questions! She needed more time to think of what questions she was supposed to ask. And she should pray about this, right? For a week at least. Being impulsive was the reason her face was bruised and her car was broken and her turtle was her turtle.

"I suppose that is a little unrealistic."

"Yes." She didn't even bother following it up with wait this time. "My answer is yes. I'll do it. I'll take it. Thank you. Thank you, thank you." Her mind was spinning. Her words were likely spinning, and she should fit together a few phrases that might convince this man he wasn't making a terrible decision, hiring a pitiable fool. "You can work this all out?" She nodded toward the B&B.

"Actually already cleared it through Calvin and Shawley. They work with me and a bunch of the churches around here all the time to house guests and do retreats and stuff. You're good to go. I need to get back to work, but we'll talk more. You can start tomorrow if you want."

"I can start tomorrow," she whispered. Mindlessly repeating what he said did not seem the best way to convince him she was not mindless. "I know the quadratic formula," she volunteered. What? "Memorized it. In high school." Good grief. Was she actually concussed? Had the car accident irreparably damaged her brain-to-mouth filter?

His eyebrows were raised in that amazed, dubiously stunned expression that was quickly becoming familiar. "Good? That'll come in handy. Math."

"Math." She nodded.

It was better for her to mindlessly repeat him until her filter healed.

CHAPTER TEN

"Jay! Dude!" If there was one thing better than hearing his best friend call out his name and stand-in name, it was the words that followed in an accidentally borderline-offensive Italian accent. "I broughta da pizza! We eata pizza for-a da dinna!"

Jay felt the tired muscles in his face stretch into a smile. Kent and Kariss were heading toward him across the lobby, holding hands as usual. Their little blond almost-four-year-old walked next to them, hands in his pockets, taking it all in with his typically serious expression.

"What did we say about you and accents?" Jay reminded as Kent set the pizza box on the desk. Ooh. Bacon smell.

"I can only do a Midwestern American one convincingly!" Then he gave his wife a high five.

Jay flipped the box open. Beef, bacon, and mushrooms. "Midwest America does not deserve you."

Kent nodded, either because he agreed or because he wasn't listening anymore. He picked up his son and settled him on his shoulders. Once the kid had a good grip on his forehead, Kent hopped up to sit on the desk. Kariss tore off a piece of her slice of pizza and handed it to the little guy. Kent wearing their child as a hat was not an uncommon sight for anyone.

"How you doing, JJ?" Jay asked his little buddy.

"Saul's daughter hated King David because he was dancing with all his might, and the ark of the cuh-neh-vant, but he was dancing because of the Lord, and she never even had any kids after that," JJ rattled off coolly, studying his pizza. Then he set his chin down on top of Kent's head and pulled pieces of bacon off his slice, popping them in his mouth one by one, apparently disinterested in everything else about pizza.

Kent grinned, eyes pointing upward. "So then what'd you do today?"

JJ smiled the black cat smile he could only have inherited from his mother. The one that hinted at dimples and was scarily endearing. "We danced with all our might." He said it with extra emphasis on the t sound and all the righteous satisfaction a three-year-old could possess.

"That sounds like the best Bible study time ever." The pizza was still hot and melty and perfect. Between the first and second bite, Jay realized he was starving.

Had he had lunch today? Oh yeah. The ladies from the Methodist church had held a brunch thing in the gym. They were fantastic, and he'd skimmed from a leftover fruit tray in between hanging Mary's banners in the hallways and leading a coaches' meeting for the softball league.

Piper had been helpful with the banners. The woman had a leveling app on her phone. She hadn't even had to download it for the purpose of hanging the banners. She just had it on her phone. They didn't use it because who had time for all that, but it was nice to know he was working with a person who had a level app on her phone "just in case." It didn't hurt having one more thing to tease her about either.

She hadn't been as much help in the softball meeting. Apparently sports were not her forte. Speaking of… "What time is it?"

Kariss checked her pocket watch. "I have 18:45."

Kent shook his head. "That's a year, babe," he said gently.

So, fifteen minutes til seven. And it was Thursday. And Cam had already skeetered out early. It would've been nice if Cam had at least stayed to introduce Piper to everyone, but it was obvious the man had all but checked out. This…this might be very interesting. "Oh boy." Jay fished his phone out of his pocket and fired off a text.

Me:

>> Come to the lobby?

"What'd you forget?" Kent asked around a mouthful of pizza. He held his slice above his head, and JJ happily stole his bacon.

Jay waved them off. A second later his phone dinged.

Swampy:

>> << Be there in a sec.

"She's quick at texting," Jay mused.

"Who?" Kent asked.

"You know the girl who brought her car to you the other day? The wrecked one? She just signed on to work here. Through the summer or until I can hire someone else full time."

Anyone to witness Kent's facial expression would've thought he'd just been told he'd won a billion dollars and the throne of some island kingdom. "Dude! You hired Piper? And she's staying in town? Awesome! So wait, are you in love with her?"

The question couldn't even surprise him anymore. "No."

Kent reached for Kariss's hand. She wore a smug expression while his looked suggestive. "But you like, like her like her?" Kent asked.

"Why do you think I'm in love with every single woman under forty that I've said two words to?"

"So she's single?" Kent did a great big, bottom-lip-between-his-teeth smile and nodded, not subtly. He'd never done anything subtly.

"Unbelievable."

Kent's eyes grew larger with every question he asked. "Does she love Jesus? Are you gonna date her? Have you asked her to go with you for coffee? That's the thing. That's what the cool guys do. When I asked Kariss out, I went, 'Hey, girl. How about coffee? And you know what we could have for dessert? Maybe like a solid future marriage modeled after the way Christ loves the church.' I was very nervous. It slipped out, you know? But it worked. She totally went for it. Later on I mean. After I reined it back a little and made an effort to come across less creepy."

Kariss deadpanned, "I liked the creepiness."

Jay took a slow breath. "I know all of that story is true, but I want you to know none of that story makes sense."

They gazed at one another like it didn't matter they were in a public place or that Kent had a small boy on his head and pizza bacon in his hair.

"I'm here. What's up? Oh, pizza." Piper seemed very pleased at the prospect as she approached. "Pizza for me?" she asked hopefully. Then seemed to think it awkward to ask and amended, "For everyone? Community pizza? Am I among the intended recipients for this pizza?" She made a face like nothing was going according to plan.

"Piper!" Kent grinned. "Hi! Yes, have pizza. This is JJ, my son." He pointed expressively upward. "You remember when I told you about JJ?"

"I do." She gave JJ a friendly wave and said, "You've got a birthday coming up in six and a half weeks. Bet you're excited."

JJ nodded without comment.

Piper took a bite of pizza then remembered the message she needed to deliver. She waited until she'd swallowed before telling Jay, "Some kids were running upstairs, and I think they ran into each other. One of them was crying. Nobody seemed injured. But I didn't know what to do about a child crying. So I gave her Skittles from the bowl in your office. Was that the right thing?"

"If that worked, then yes. Did I happen to mention that part of your job involves coaching one of the boys' basketball teams?"

The pizza slice froze halfway to her mouth. "Coaching a what?"

"And did I mention that you've got about ten fifth and sixth grade boys who will be in that gym in, oh, around ten minutes or so, ready for you to coach them for an hour?"

Her open mouth fell open farther. "Huh?"

"Basketball. Ten- or eleven-year-old boys. You'll be great. A lot of them have played before. It's just a summer community program, not real competitive. Just, you know, teach them the fundamentals and try to keep them from running into each other. It'll be a lot of fun."

"I...I...I..."

"She doesn't look very confident," Kent observed. Kariss chewed pizza with her eyes on them like she was watching a movie.

"I can't coach basketball! Where's Cam? He still works here until tomorrow. That is in his contract! Right? Is there a contract? Is there even like an assistant coach? An assistant coach who could do most of the... coaching?"

Jay tried to replace all his amusement with apology. "Nope, sorry. Cam's gone, and you're it."

"No! I will kill Cam." She looked up at JJ and backpedaled. "Oh. Sorry. I'm not really going to kill anyone. Killing is wrong. Don't ever...do it." Having reinforced the sixth Commandment, she turned back to Jay. "You don't understand. I don't know anything about basketball! My entire repository of basketball knowledge pretty much begins and ends in the late 90s with how Aaron Carter 'beat Shaq.'"

Inexplicably, Kariss spoke up with, "Boom."

"Boom!" Piper echoed, hands in the air. In keeping with the general theme of Jay's experience with her—a mess of cheese and toppings flew off her pizza and landed in the path of a stampede of sweaty eighth graders who'd just finished their own basketball practice. Jay winced. Piper looked from her topping-less crust to the saucy mess being tracked across the lobby. All she did was sigh.

"You got this," Jay encouraged. He walked around the desk and patted her upper arm as he passed.

"I'm gonna go print off your roster. You finish eating and head to the gym. Parents are going to drop their kids off pretty soon, so you'll want to introduce yourself."

"I'm coming with you to print it!" Kent volunteered before she could answer and hopped off the desk.

JJ, visibly unbothered by the jostling of his perch, reached out and latched onto Jay's shoulder, tugging until Jay got close enough for the little guy to wrap his arms around Jay's neck. He transferred from his Pop's shoulders to his Uncle Jay's back with the fearless grace of a koala bear.

With the ease of much practice, Jay adjusted the grip around his neck so he could breathe and caught the spindly little legs clinging at his waist. "We'll be right back," he promised. "Just running into the main office real quick," and he was sure, he was positive, it wasn't cruel to want to laugh at the look on Piper's face right then. A few years ago, he and Kent had gone skydiving. A kid in their group wore an expression just like that the moment the instructor opened the airplane door.

In a moment of blessed tact, Kent waited until they were out of earshot before asking, "So Piper, though?"

"Piper, though."

"How'd she do today?"

"Good. Cam trained her a lot of the day. He said she was fine. From what I saw, she was fine."

"And you're not in love with her at all?"

97

"Nope," he confirmed as they reached the office door. It was locked, and the lights were out.

"But you like her."

"Oh, she's hilarious." He pulled JJ around to the front so he could hold him in one arm while he dug his keys out of his pocket. JJ scowled as the door opened and wriggled until he could crawl back around to cling to Jay's back unaided. *With all the fearless grace of an angry koala bear.* "If she doesn't end up quitting at the end of the day—which is not an impossibility—I think she'll do a good job. I mean, she wants to do a good job. At everything." He flipped on the lights. "She alphabetizes things and wants to know rules and procedures. She brought a notepad. To take notes. For when I 'gave her the orientation.' I think she expected a slideshow presentation or a training video or something."

Kent laughed. "Aww. You giving orientation. Dude. That is hilarious. You'd be like, 'When things happen, we deal with the things. That is the orientation.' And your presentation would be like one slide with a gif of a fire hydrant that's on fire."

"Right? Apparently she's got secretarial, office type experience, which is perfect to help me out, but probably means it's going to drive her crazy to work here. But we'll see. She's got…something. I don't know what it is. But she's got it."

"Is it moxie?" Kent asked, entirely too seriously.

Jay considered that. "You know how, traditionally, they say ladies are made of sugar and spice and everything nice?"

"Yeah."

"This woman is like sugar and disaster and everything...fierce."

Kent made an open-mouthed excited face. "I'm not clear on the exact definition of moxie, but I hope it's that!"

"Oh, I have to tell you about the turtle."

CHAPTER ELEVEN

It took a little longer to print out the roster than Jay planned. It was more due to Kent and his son both being three year olds playing with the copier than anything else. Kariss had smiled at Jay when she'd come to collect her boys. It always made him nervous when she smiled at him. As he walked into the gym, he saw ten fifth and sixth graders laughing and shouting and having a great time with basketballs. And he saw Piper Cope standing inches off one of the free throw lines looking strangely serene and not at all in charge.

Jay was careful in his approach. "Hey there."

She made a small noise of acknowledgment.

"Printed the thing."

She made no move to take the roster. It was a beat before she spoke. "I had it under control," she said, her voice soft and reflective and confused. "In the beginning. They were in a line. All four thousand of them. It was a straight line, Jay."

"Mmhm. That's fine." He kept his voice even and supportive in deference to her apparent trauma. "Then what happened?"

"One of them farted," she replied. "I don't...I don't even know."

"Mmhm," his voice came out less even and supportive and more like he was holding back a guffaw. Which he was. "Would you like some help?"

"That woman, Katniss..."

"Nope."

"Kariss. I said Kariss, right?"

"Okay."

"She left me here with them." Her bruised eyes found his, wide and utterly betrayed. It was a look that seemed familiar, but the best he could do to place it was the expression of a little girl who'd been abandoned in a theme park full of dinosaurs.

"I help you run your practice tonight, you update the newsletter for me tomorrow?" he offered.

"Yes. A thousand times yes."

The dashboard clock glowed a green 9:26 that hurt her eyes, but she didn't have the energy to turn her head away. Or even shut her eyes. Piper knew Jay had just pulled his car up to Shawley Bea's and she would be expected to exit the vehicle. Which meant she'd very soon need to gather the willpower to move her entire being out of the car and up the steps. *Not. Possible.*

"I'm going to see about getting a vehicle you can borrow until your car's fixed."

Jay had been comfortingly silent the whole brief ride, and she'd forgotten that two humans in close proximity were expected to have conversation.

What was the proper response to the words he'd just said? *Ah, right. More words. Come on, mouth. Do words.* "Thank you."

"You gonna be okay?"

"Mm'yep."

"Good. See you tomorrow?"

"Mm'yep?" She hadn't meant to make it sound like a question. Her exhausted brain had seen fit to mimic the upward lilt at the end of his sentence. "Mm'yep. Thanks, Jay. God bless you."

"You, too, old chum," he said and bumped her elbow with his fist.

She did not whine at him. It took effort to open the door and hoist herself out of the vehicle without any embarrassing noises. She was sore. She hadn't done much that was overtly physically taxing, but everything ached.

A fun blend of post-fender bender throbbing and was-I-nervously-tensing-every-muscle-in-my-body-all-day twinginess.

Shawley and Calvin had already turned in, though they'd left the kitchen light on. Piper found a container of corn muffins on the counter and a note that read *There's chili in the fridge. Hope your first day went well!* signed with a heart and an S.

In fourth grade, Piper had a friend whose mom always left her notes on index cards in her lunch. Shawley was definitely the kind of mom who would've left notes on index cards in her kids' lunches.

She stuck the note in the pocket of her shorts and took two muffins and a leaf off the head of lettuce in the fridge. She was hungry, but chili sounded like the last thing she wanted. The banister played a major role in her trip up the stairs. The house stayed hushed as she crossed through her room to the bath and sat on the toilet lid. Her shoulders slumped forward of their own accord, and it felt wonderful. She pulled one knee up, then caught motion out of the corner of her eye.

"Hey, Hubcaptain."

He was sitting on his floating turtle dock, basking under his lamp like a great armored princess. With his gravel-lined tub and his fancy habitat accessories. The Hayeses had both insisted on an outing to Pet Kingdom—a forty-five minute drive. Apparently the idea of not being hospitable to the wild pet of their most inconvenient guest offended them to their gooey centers. They were mind-boggling. And neither of them said a word of complaint when Piper interrogated the Pet Kingdom associate with a mortifying number of questions on turtle care. Good heavens, if I ever had actual human children, I'd be one of those mothers.

By the end, Piper had, in deference to her bank account, bought the bare essentials to ensure a healthy pet. Shawley and Calvin bought him toys.

Piper handed Hubs the lettuce leaf and took a bite of her muffin. She didn't say anything else. He, being a turtle, didn't either. After a day of being constantly, overwhelmingly surrounded by a thousand unfamiliar voices and tasks, she was surprised to find herself grateful for the company. Didn't even seem odd that she was dozing off on the toilet with her chin on her knee.

CHAPTER TWELVE

Seven-thirty felt excruciatingly early Saturday morning when Piper clumsily managed to open the door while balancing her turtle carrier. Her basketball team—she was still getting used to the idea that she had a basketball team—had a game every Saturday. This particular Saturday, they'd landed in the first slot. Eight a.m. Normally eight a.m. wouldn't phase her, but after the previous evening's movie night at the community center, she'd spent an irresponsible amount of time looking up information on North American painted turtles and DIYing a custom carrier. She didn't regret her actions. She briefly regretted her actions for a few moments around the time her alarm went off that morning. But for the most part, she didn't regret her actions.

She spotted Jay beelining it for the gym with the quick, purposeful stride she'd already learned to recognize as his autopilot. He must've seen her with his peripheral vision, because a second later he leaned backwards out the gym's double doors to stare at her. "What is that?" Apparently it was peculiar enough to warrant him backing out of the gym to walk toward her.

"I made it," Piper said proudly. It had started as a 12" x 24" wooden flower tray from the shed by the garden at Shawley's. It had six-inch slats that rose from the base to create a nice enclosure, and she'd lined the inside with plastic and made a little turtle paradise. Then she'd attached a fabric strap, in a lovely green and blue paisley, so she could cart it around like a popcorn peddler at a ballgame. The whole thing was honestly pretty adorable, and she didn't think she was being biased.

She still wanted to paint the outside of the wood. Something that would coordinate well with the paisley print but that would befit a turtle as masculine and brawny as Hubcap. "This turtle is now ultra-mobile."

"You brought your turtle." It wasn't a question. But it was very nearly a question.

"Of course."

"To a basketball game."

"Yeah. I felt bad leaving him at home alone all day again. Originally I thought I could get one of those strap-on baby carriers, but according to my research, it's not good for turtles to be kept vertical like that for extended periods of time."

"How heavy is the box?" Then he shook his head like that wasn't what he'd meant to say. "Piper, you can't have this thing here. What if it bites a kid or something?"

106

"First of all, he would never do that. Second of all, according to my research, he might scratch a kid. So keep all the kids away from him."

Jay sucked in a breath and puffed his cheeks out for a second, rolling his eyes back toward the gym and, presumably, whatever he'd been on his way to do. "Don't let him harm any children. And make sure nobody on your team is allergic to turtles."

"You can have a turtle allergy?" She raised an eyebrow, but he was already moving back toward the gym. She raised her voice after him, "Because according to…"

"If you say 'according to my research' one more time, you're fired," he fairly sang back over his shoulder.

She grinned.

The gym wasn't as noisy as Piper thought it would be. There were two basketball games going on at once, one on each half of the court. They'd set up four rolling, semi-collapsible hoops to create the two courts, separated by a line of folding chairs set back to back along the half court line to act as benches for the players and coaches. Which meant there was a game happening in front of her and a game happening behind her and parent/guardians scattered around in the stands and referees with whistles around their necks. Tons of basketball everywhere. But it wasn't that loud. Not loud enough to completely drown out the sound of her nerves buzzing under her skin, in point of fact.

She hadn't been aware nervousness had a sound, but she was pretty certain when she stopped to concentrate on how far out of her depths she was, she could hear the faint twang of tense muscles and tendons and various ligaments. Strumming like a bluegrass band. Sounded like the opening licks of "Man of Constant Sorrows" actually.

That seemed more like imagination than science. *Yeah, I should've gotten more sleep.*

She focused on the freckled boy standing before her flicking his dark bangs out of his eyes and asking to go to the bathroom. He had a name. Piper did not know what it was. She wasn't entirely sure she had ever seen him before. But his reversible jersey was turned to the same blue as all the rest of her team. It had a number 45 on it and, like the others, the SBCC logo but no last name. Where was her clipboard? She'd just had her roster clipboard, hadn't she?

To be fair, he probably didn't know her name either. He'd addressed her as "Coach." Ha. Obviously he didn't know her at all.

He was ten or eleven. That was old enough not to need to take a parent with him to go to the bathroom, right? What were the rules on that? She wasn't sure about how kids worked. "Yes. Go ahead. Take a buddy with you." Buddy system. That seemed safe.

"Who? Chase?" he asked.

Which one was Chase? There were four other boys on the bench. A nondescript brunette doing something with a smartphone—kids today with their smartphones. *Where did that come from? How old am I?* Next to him, a lighter brunette, slightly nuggety, who was only a few inches shorter than Piper. Then there were two blonds who, now that she was looking at them, might be twins. She thought one of their names was Jasper. No, that wasn't right. Oh, for all she knew, both their names were Jasper.

"Sure," she said carefully.

The dark-haired boy nodded and stepped up to the line taped down on the floor and cupped his hands over his mouth. "Chase!" and waved one of the players over.

A short African American boy with close-cropped hair looked over from where he was guarding one of the other team's players. He shrugged and started jogging over. Applause erupted as the other team scored with their extra man.

"No, no!" Piper called, waving her arms. "No, Chase. Keep playing, man! You're doing great!" She gave him a thumbs up and turned to the bathroom kid. "You have to choose a buddy from the bench."

"Can I choose the turtle?" He eyeballed Hubcap's carrier she'd tucked under the bench.

"A human. You have to choose a human buddy."

"Why?" He waved his hands. "Everything is rules!" Unexplainable fury built across his brow like a thundercloud.

Zero to hopping mad in 0.7 seconds flat. Oh, dear. Not that she couldn't relate. But she had no idea how to deal with an angry ten-year-old. And furthermore, the game wasn't half over yet, her team was down by 21 points because of that showoff on the other team, there were parents in the stands forming opinions of her—correct ones at that—Smartphone on the bench over there was probably live-Tweeting this whole disastrous affair, and now Thundercloud was putting out enough negative energy to upset meteorological equipment in the next county.

But at least she knew Chase's name. One down.

She looked into the irate young face before her. Her problem-solving and communication skills amounted to, "Wuh-ahhhhhhh…?"

"Noah. What's going on, man?" A stern, even, still-somehow-friendly voice nearly made her jump. She turned to find Jay Marler had materialized. She was torn between relief and embarrassment.

"I have to go to the bathroom!" he complained loudly.

"Basic human need," Jay agreed reasonably. "So what's the problem?"

"She won't let me go unless I go with somebody. It's stupid."

"Whoa. Hey, nope. Not okay. At all."

As Piper watched, something about the intensity of Jay's gaze or disappointment or mysterious superpowers caused the boy to shrink and cross his arms, noisy anger morphing into quiet defensiveness.

"That's your coach," Jay said. "And a person, by the way. You know a whole lot better than to talk like that to her or about her. If she said to go with somebody, you say 'Yes, ma'am,' and make it happen. And while you're gone, I'm gonna need you to crank the attitude back about ten notches. That's not how we do it here."

"But…" Thundercloud—Noah. Oh, hey, that's ironic!—began like he expected to be interrupted. Jay remained unmoved.

"Fine," Noah said. He exchanged a brief few words with the possible-twin on the end of the row. The blond stood up and waved at them before the two made their way around the edge of the court to the exit.

"Noah's usually fine," Jay said like he hadn't just slightly saved the day. "Kid's just been on a hair trigger lately. I need to talk to his dad later."

She glanced at Jay, standing next to her. "You know, if you'd been born in a different time you could've been burned at the stake for that sort of magic."

He gave a quick, wide grin. "How's it going?"

"Abysmally I think," she answered in merry tones over the sound of the crowd cheering as the opposing team scored yet again and her boys looked the slightest

111

bit unhappier. "It's all right guys! You got this! Keep on… keeping on." She lowered her head and her voice without pausing for breath before again owning the fact that, "I am not good at coaching basketball."

"Really? You were fine at practice the other night." Jay turned to her bench and its three remaining players. "Hey, guys, what have you learned from Coach Cope today?"

The big kid raised a fist and said, "'Slow and steady wins the race!'" with no lack of enthusiasm.

Smartphone didn't look up when he answered, "Turtles are omnivores. They eat plants and animals both."

The remaining maybe-a-twin looked vaguely alarmed. He recovered quickly. "Tortoises live on land!"

Jay crossed his arms and lowered a glare Piper's direction.

She popped her lips. "You know. We've mostly talked about Hubcap today." Amid strict instructions not to touch. "They were interested. It was educational. Turtles are an important part of the ecosystem. According to my…" She paused as his raised eyebrow reminded her that phrase was off-limits. *How often did she say according to my research?* "According to my exploratory study…" Not much better. "I'll stop talking."

His mouth twisted into a calculating, got-a-lemon-on-my-tongue expression that came complete with one squinting eye. She hoped it meant he was more amused than annoyed. "'Slow and steady wins the race'?" he repeated slowly. Definitely amused then.

"I've been reading up on turtles a lot. I was trying to find a turtle anecdote that applied to sports."

"That one does not apply to basketball."

"Got it. Hey, team!" she called. "Eighty-six the 'slow and steady' thing! Just basketball!" She made a twirling motion with her hand, indicating that "basketball" was an action verb. "Basketball faster!"

"Not necessarily wrong." Jay stuck his hands in his pockets. "But thoroughly unhelpful."

Do kids know what 86 means? "'86' means to discontinue something!" The other team scored again while her team was distracted. By her. She kept a rigid smile in place as she dropped her head. "I really don't know what I'm doing. You seem not worried that I might be ruining these children's lives and their basketball educations."

She felt herself working up a good rant. She tried to stop it. But in the end it was too powerful. "I don't know any of their names. Except Chase. And Noah now. I'm pretty sure there are precious few of them who like me at all. Precious fewer of the parents. And they're not wrong. This is not a setting in which I am likable. I don't get little boys. I don't get sports. I did marching band in high school. And we weren't even good. I don't have that tone of voice you have that makes kids like, 'Yes, he is my authority figure and my friend, and he will have my obedience and my sworn allegiance for all time.' Where do you get that? Is there like an online course? Or some sort of potion maybe?"

"No."

Piper waited. There seemed to be no follow up. "Well. Okay then."

"Piper. This isn't the big time." He leaned his head nearer. Was he going to use his magic voice on her? She expected to be more immune to it than an eleven year old.

"Just hang in there. You'll be fine. The reason I'm not worried is that this isn't something to worry about. Honestly. It's a fun thing. It's exercise and light competition and something to do with the summer break. It's not going to matter who wins. Have fun. Let them have fun. They're people, too."

Piper took a deep breath. Everything smelled like hotdogs and nachos and little boy sweat. "Children are people, too," she repeated. "That is some groundbreaking thinking actually."

"Isn't it? Even more so than 'Slow and steady wins the race.'"

"So we're not gonna let that one go. Excellent."

"I don't see how we can. I'm wiser than Aesop. That's what we learned here." He pointed at her and commissioned, "Learn the names of your team."

"Good advice."

He crossed to the bleachers and sat next to a middle-aged woman near the top. The two immediately engaged in conversation.

This isn't the big time. She looked around the gym. Each side had a folding table with a timekeeper and a scorekeeper for their assigned game. Apparently the big scoreboard had been on the fritz for a good four or five years. The referees were not wearing striped shirts. She had been certain up to this point that referees were supposed to wear striped shirts. The one officiating her team's game wore a dark purple shirt from a high school's production of Les Mis and looked seventeen. Not the big time. Maybe it didn't matter she wasn't good at coaching basketball? Maybe she could just be a purveyor of fun. Was basketball even fun?

Noah and the blond, twinnish boy skipped back from their trek to the bathroom and flopped into their chairs, talking loudly and laughing.

Smartphone, sitting nearest her, glanced over briefly and then returned to whatever brightly-colored game he was playing. She leaned over him and asked, "Hey, what's the blond kid's name?"

"Which one?" he asked.

"The one who just got back from the bathroom."

"Kollin."

"Are he and the other one twins?"

"Yeah."

"What's the other one's name?"

"Kolby."

Kollin and Kolby. Aw. "You know their last name?"

"Jasper."

Ha! "Nailed it!" She only barely managed to avoid a fist pump. And only then because Smartphone gave her a remarkably adult-like expression of concern over her sanity. She cleared her throat. "You want to go in and play basketball next?" she asked as a thank you for his help.

He appeared unimpressed by the offer. It occurred to her he hadn't even taken his jacket off. Apparently she wasn't the only one who didn't get basketball. The sudden sense of camaraderie helped. She hadn't expected to be able to feel camaraderie with a ten- or eleven-year-old person.

"Nah. You can send in Dillon." He indicated the tall boy beside him with a tilt of his head. "Or Kollin."

The other four on the bench must've overheard the exchange because then it was a frenzy of "I wanna go," and "I'll do it," and, most succinctly, "Me."

She looked at all of their faces and shrugged. "Sure. Why not." She called for a substitution next chance she got. Switched everybody out except Chase because she knew his name and spent the next half of the game alternating among telling the bench crew that the turtle might attack them like a wild animal if they touched him, downloading the game Smartphone was playing so she could join his band of Vikings, and calling out helpful playing tips to her players such as, "You're doing great!" and "Get the—you know—basketball!"

CHAPTER THIRTEEN

The next week flew by in a frenzy of fast-paced, impossible hours and organizing a thousand things flawlessly while somehow managing to misplace her SBCC ID an estimated twenty-one times. She always managed to find it in the end.

Piper had managed to get into a groove at the community center, gotten a feel for the office, worked out the cadence to her "Silas Bend Community Center, this is Piper," phone greeting. People were beginning to recognize her as a fixture. Someone to be asked questions. A responsible party. And she was becoming accustomed to getting to the end of the day and feeling mentally and physically spent. At any other point in her life, Piper would've found the routine punishing.

It was nice, though. Actually. In a way. Sunday had been a true day off, and she'd gone to church with Shawley and Calvin. Rode in the backseat, feeling like a little girl, but delighted they'd invited her. She'd done service and Sunday school, and Jay and the Peepers had been present and welcoming. In Kent's case, loudly welcoming, but she was becoming accustomed to that, too. Lunch afterwards with the Hayeses was apparently something of a tradition. All of it was lovely.

Sunday evening, though, she'd been on her own. While she would've thought that would be exactly what she wanted, she'd found the quiet and stillness of her room a little too…quiet and still. Without the constant everything, she was left with only her thoughts. She thought she'd been fine. But in the quiet, it was different. Among irritation and lingering bitterness and the acrid stench of injustice, her thoughts had turned unexpectedly sad.

Her finger felt unbalanced without the weight of the engagement ring. Mark's eyes had gone bright with tears as he looked up at her from his place down on his knee, and she hadn't thought he'd be the type to react that way. They'd made her feel so special, those tears. She'd expected the ring and its diamond. His tears, though. They'd been proof that his love was right. Real. Profound. Undeniable.

She couldn't remember exactly what Mark said to her when he proposed. Weren't girls supposed to remember that forever? She remembered thinking she would. Of course she would. Not that it mattered. It was probably a blessing, then. Not to remember the words of promise spoken by the man she never married.

In her room on Sunday evening, she'd been disgusted with herself. Because she shouldn't miss him.

118

She should be furious with him. Or she should have forgiven him already and moved on. And yet…

She felt very, very sad. And more than a little distressed that it wasn't Mark she missed as much as the future he'd promised her.

There was something about being very, very sad in a room by herself in a town full of near-to-complete strangers. Something about looking through the contacts in her phone and, for each name, being able to think of a reason why she shouldn't send a text or hit "call" to tell any one of them, I feel very, very sad. Something that made her chest heavy and her shoulders ache. The tears she cried spoke of weakness rather than grief.

She'd tried to pray. It didn't seem that any of her prayers made sense.

She didn't want to spend another evening that way. So when Jay told her, "You don't have to come on the bike thing on Saturday. Unless you want to. It's gonna be fun," she had immediately agreed. Biking wasn't like basketball. She knew how to ride a bike. It had been a while. But the expression literally went, "It's like riding a bike."

She "coached" her basketball team through another crushing defeat Saturday morning. They couldn't have done it without her. But! She had taught the little redhead named Wayne that turtle shells are made up of sixty different bones connected together. Knowledge is power. If power translated into basketball prowess, her team would be unstoppable.

Piper waited for Jay. He had a seventh and eighth grade boys' team that practiced Wednesday nights. His team also lost their Saturday game, though by a much thinner margin. They would've won if they'd had the power of turtle facts.

"You ready to go?" Jay asked. He'd procured a vehicle for her to drive. A white Buick Park Avenue from the mid-90s that got her to and from work and had a tape deck. *A tape deck.* But Jay's car had a bike rack. And when he offered her rides, she took him up on it, if for no other reason than it saved on gas and she didn't have to worry about running into any trees to avoid reptiles.

He'd also procured a bike for her to ride. A lovely pink-and-black affair, dusty and neglected, but with a gear shift and a place for a water bottle. Perfectly efficient.

"So where did these sweet wheels come from?"

"Mary."

"Ah. Always?"

"I have an embarrassing level of reliance on her, yes."

The bike adventurers met together near the entrance of Chimney Ridge Park, a parking lot near a playground old enough to have a merry-go-round. A hearty group of ten women and eight men, Kent and Kariss among them. Beyond the playground, a narrow asphalt road led deeper into the park. She couldn't tell how far it went. There were quite a few trees. A whole forest of them, with trails cut through for walking or biking.

Piper felt inexplicably nervous. Well, slightly explicably. Trail riding seemed a lot like something one needed a certain level of coordination for. And while there was a time in her life it would not have intimidated her, her coordination track record of late was not encouraging.

Seems like there should be someone to stay by the cars. People have coolers and stuff. Those could attract... raccoons. Or bears. Yes, definitely someone should stay behind and guard the food that's inside the coolers that are inside the cars. Oh, yes. Yes, that sounded perfectly reasonable and not at all ridiculous. Since her arrival in Silas Bend, she had yet to manage walking through nature without winding up filthy, soaked, humiliated, and/or mildly injured.

"You look...contemplative," Jay said as he pulled her bike off the rack and set it on the ground.

"Trying to calculate the odds of me managing to pilot a two-wheeled, manual, personal transport machine through a park for a few hours without causing major damage to my person or anyone else's...person."

"Shockingly not an instance when it pays to have the quadratic formula memorized?"

She felt her face go flat, and turned to fix her look on him and his teasing, not-quite grin. All it did was undo the "not-quite" setting on his grin.

"Jay! Pi!" Kent bounded up, followed by Kariss stepping up next to him at a less boundy pace. Her auburn hair had been tied up in a complicated bun with a series of tiny braids. She managed to look simultaneously classy and carefree in her open flannel shirt and tank top and shorts. She tipped her chin in a cool, salutatory half-nod.

Piper tried the half-nod, but didn't think she could pull it off. She had not a fifth of the coolness. "Hello, Peepers."

"Dude! I got a write-up in the *Chronicle*!" Kent said, with all his usual excitement and then some. "Did you see it? I mean, not me. Well, yeah, me. Peeper's Auto, though. We're totally in the paper. You saw it, right?"

Jay rubbed his chin. "Hm. Well. I can't be sure, but I think you texted me about that today."

"I did! Yes!" Kent gestured at his chest with both arms. "That was me!"

"About twenty-five times."

"Exactly twenty-five times!"

"You know, I did see that in the paper today." Jay sounded proud as he smacked his friend's shoulder. "Way to go. It was perfect."

"This lady just came in and was like, 'Oh, I'm from the *Silas Bend Chronicle*, and we're doing something-something about local businesses, and is it okay if I asked you about your business?' And so I was like, 'Of course you can!' Dude, did you read it, though?"

"I really did. It was awesome. She said some nice things. Really nice. That's going to be so good for business. People read that paper, man."

"I didn't see it," Piper said. "What'd she say?"

Kent's triumphant smile could have easily guided weary, seagoing vessels. Even this far from any actual sea. "I've got bon homie!"

Piper glanced at Jay, who seemed the same level of stumped as she. "Sorry?"

"That's one of the things she said. In the article. She said the owner, Kent Peeper, has an 'exuberant style of customer service and a rare, possibly unparalleled bon homie.' And I'm just thinking, wow. What an honor."

Bon homie. Ohh. "I think the word is bonhomie," Piper broke the news gently.

Kent looked at her uncomprehendingly. "What?" with all his emphasis on the t sound.

"Bonhomie. Like, intense friendliness. Good-natured. That sort of...thing."

Kent clicked his tongue and held up one finger. "I have been saying it wrong," he declared. "I was going to say, you're all my bon homies. Especially you, babe," to Kariss. "But," his expression grew serious and speechy, "since now I know what it means and how to say it—thanks, Pi—let me just say this: you are all the best people. Ever. Especially you, babe," again, to Kariss. "You are the best wife who has ever lived. And Jay. You know you're my brother, dude. And Piper. I realize we just met, but it was your cruddy car in my shop that I was working on when the lady came in, so you're totally involved. I never could've done this without all of you.

And I mean that from the bottom of my heart. From bonhomie to bonhoyou."

Piper had to chew hard on her lips to keep a straight face.

"Well said," Jay nodded solemnly.

This. This was what Jay needed. A night out riding a bike up and down trails, sun beating down, wind in his face, dirt and rocks whizzing by under him. Kent barely visible up ahead, hollering as he took his bike off a frankly absurd jump.

He hardly felt the light burn in his quads over the beat of his heart in his chest.

"Hey."

Jay glanced over his left shoulder to see Piper, puffing along behind him, keeping up gamely, a spark of humor hanging around her eyes. *Well, look who's having a good time.* He angled his bike to the right. The trail was narrow, but there was space enough she could bring herself up next to him. "Look at you."

"I know!" She seemed very pleased with herself. And surprised. "I'm kind of awesome at mountain biking."

"You know, you are. It's impressive."

124

"It is shocking! I haven't even fallen down. Not one time."

"None of the local fauna, nor flora, have tried to attack you yet?"

"None."

Her smile was contagious, framed by strands of her dark hair, fallen loose and blowing back in the wind. Reminded him of the day he'd met her. Not in a bad way.

"Ha! Come at me, trees!"

Jay laughed but didn't say anything for a moment. He looked ahead. They'd almost reached the jump Kent took. Normally Jay wouldn't try it. He wasn't that guy. He glanced at Piper again. For whatever reason, absurd started to look appealing.

He grinned at her and then cut over, increasing his speed and aiming for the jump. Just a hill of packed dirt, man-made and probably not near as big as it looked. *It looked pretty big. Decently big. Not, not that big.*

"Are you kidding me?" he heard Piper call behind him.

Through a sudden surge of adrenaline, of the tug-and-pull of the mostly-subconscious battle between this is not a good idea and this is a great idea, he felt the front tire hit the incline, and he shifted his weight from his hands to his feet just before the front of the bike went airborne. The back followed, and he was flying, totally unattached to the ground. Focused on traveling in a straight line. His heart and stomach attempted to switch places.

His knees and hands took the impact as he landed, slightly off-balance, and panic struck as his handlebars wobbled. There was a brief interval when he was sure he was going to wipe out. But he pulled it out, swung the bike around, and skidded to a stop, managing somehow (*thank you, Lord!*) to stay upright.

Jay managed to keep his relief silent as he wiped sweat from his eyes with the back of his hand. That was awesome. Kent was not wrong. That was awesome. He only wanted to do that never again and a thousand more times. Leaning toward a thousand more times.

"Jay." He looked up at Kariss's sharp voice. Grim, she stood next to her bike several yards up the trail. From Jay's position he could just make out one of Piper's red tennis shoes sticking out from behind the foliage near Kariss's foot.

Oh no. Suddenly the adrenaline was back, but it was not fun. Jay dumped his bike and sprinted toward them. He slowed when he heard Piper's voice.

"Don't call him over here. Are you kidding me?"

He approached the scene with caution. As he neared Kariss and the red shoe, he had to clear his throat. "Are you okay?" he asked.

"Fine! Fine. Move along, please. I'll be right behind you."

It was at that point he allowed himself a smile. To be honest, the smile was happening whether he allowed it or not. "Piper," he said diplomatically. "How…How?"

She was on the ground just next to the trail. She'd come all the way off the bike. Which, very likely would have been okay if it hadn't been for the fact that this girl...this woman...had somehow gotten her long, dark hair very much wrapped up in her bike chain. Impossibly wrapped up in her bike chain. She was trapped. He'd looked away for ten seconds, and she was trapped by her hair.

"I seem to have fallen," she said slowly through gritted teeth.

Don't you dare say it.

"It appears," she added, no less unhappily, "that I cannot get up."

Jay very nearly lost it at that point.

"Don't you laugh!"

"You can't..." he snickered through his protest, "You can't just say something like that and tell me not to laugh."

"I can!" She tugged ineffectually at the mess of hair tangled in the bike chain. "You could at least have the decency to pretend to be coughing!"

"I wouldn't want to worry you. In the movies, you know if a character's coughing, they're obviously dying. Coughing. It's like a death knell."

"You wanna hear a death knell?" she threatened.

Jay glanced at Kariss. She looked as amused as she ever could, and he answered, "Okay."

Piper drew in a dramatic breath. As dramatic as he assumed she could while lying on the ground with a bike stuck in her hair. "I don't actually have a follow up for that. Help me. Help me, please."

CHAPTER FOURTEEN

They'd ended up having to cut it. *To cut it. Her hair. Not the bike chain.* Jay and Kariss had tried taking the chain off the bike to free her, but no. It was no good. She'd gotten tangled around the crankset, and ouch, and they'd had to cut her out. She'd had to lie in the dirt, trying to keep still while Jay Marler sawed off hunks of her hair with a Swiss Army knife. Also, her ponytail holder had snapped.

Piper sat at a picnic table in the park. Post-bike ride, everyone gathered round a fire pit for a bonfire. It seemed a bit small to be considered a bonfire, but it worked for their purposes. A bonhomie fire, then. Good for hotdogs and marshmallows, the usual fare. She had a plate in front of her with ketchup smears and potato chip crumbs, and a kind stranger from the bike troupe was sitting across from her telling her it really didn't look so bad.

"Sort of edgy. You know. You look super hard-core." The girl looked a little younger than Piper.

"Thank you?"

"And with your eyes all...the way they are, it makes a statement."

"Is it a good statement?"

The stranger tilted her head and paused long enough to answer without saying a word.

Piper reached across and patted her hand. "It's okay. I appreciate you trying."

The girl's sympathetic expression seemed less pained as she stood. "I'm going to go make a s'more. Want one?"

"No, thank you." Why wasn't Piper more upset about the fall, the devil bicycle chain, losing the bulk of her hair? Was she in shock? Possible. But as she dismissed the girl and her offer with an aristocratic wave of the hand, she was proud of herself that she hadn't met this new catastrophe with a wild desire to hunt anything.

Jay appeared, sliding into the girl's vacated place on the bench seat. He dropped a dingy-white, scuffed-up baseball cap on the table between them. "I found that. In my car. If you know anyone... Obviously you don't need a hat at all. Or, I mean, you don't need one. If you would like one, however, if it would make you feel better, then...here's one. It's used, but also...unwashed. Sorry."

His tone of voice was the awkward one he used when he wasn't sure whether or not he might offend her.

It was more comfortable now, though. More like gentle teasing than actual uncertainty. He certainly hadn't been worried about offending her when he'd been laughing at her plight or hacking away at her hair.

She gathered up the uneven ends of her hair and tucked them up under the hat. "I can't see what I look like. I really don't have a good hat face. But I imagine this beats a mountain bike for fashion hair accessories."

"Can't say I've ever really followed the fashion industry."

"No? And to think I let you cut my hair."

He grinned and goaded, "You should've worn a helmet."

She pointed a threatening finger. "Quiet, you."

Closer to the fire, Kent sat in a lawn chair with a guitar in his lap. He went from picking mindlessly to strumming and singing without reserve. His song choice was unfamiliar, possibly made up as he went along, but not unpleasant. The music drew people in and had them clapping along. Kariss sat next to him, her feet crossed at the ankle and resting on his free knee, flicking playing cards one by one at the fire for reasons that must have made sense to her.

Jay sat with his back to them. He didn't seem to think it unusual that his best friend would host an impromptu sing-along. Jay put his hands on the rough wooden top of the table and leaned toward her to be heard. "I still can't figure out how you managed it without pulling all your hair out of your scalp." He cringed like a boy with a skinned knee. "So there's a silver lining."

"Oh, there are plenty of upsides."

"Like what?"

"Aside from the fact that I may be developing an immunity to humiliation, due to repeated overexposure, I'll have to check my card of course, but I'm pretty sure this gives me four corners in My Life Is Actually a Sitcom BINGO."

His sudden laughter warmed her soul. "I think the boys on your basketball team will think your new 'do and the story that goes with it are awesome."

"Hm. Here's a thought. I could be our mascot." She shook her head. "No, no, no. If anyone's our mascot, it's Hubcap G. Cope. It is his animal birthright."

"What's the G stand for?"

"Haven't decided." Until that moment, she hadn't realized Hubs' middle initial was G. "Garfield?"

"Greg?" he offered.

"Gavin?"

"Grayson?"

"George?"

"Gabe?"

"Geoff?"

He raised an eyebrow at her.

"You know," she defended. "Geoff. With a G. Posh Geoff."

"Right," he conceded the point. "He is pretty posh. Glen?

"Ggggg…" she drew out, waiting for her brain to supply a name. The only thing that came to her was, "Gilmingham?"

"Not sure that's a name."

"No?"

"Not sure it's not, though," he admitted. "Garfield?"

"That was the first one I said!"

He held up his hands as though it was obvious. "Well that one's perfect."

"Hubcap Garfield Cope."

"Kind of expected you to finish with 'Esquire,'" he said.

"Hubcap Garfield Cope. Official animal representative and applause broker for Summer Basketball Team 5B, SBCC."

"Excellent. We'll get him an I.D. badge." He tapped his fingers on the tabletop. "How's that going, by the way? The coaching. Better this week?"

Better seemed very subjective. "Well, I learned their names."

"That's a start."

"And I think we're getting better at, you know, bouncing the basketballs."

He gestured at her. "And?"

"And what?"

"Where's the, 'According to my research,' etcetera, etcetera? The other day you looked up 'Best floor mopping technique' and then explained it to me. And what was the other one you did? The funny one?"

"'How to teach a North American painted turtle to play fetch'?"

"No. Well, yes. That wasn't the one I was… But does that work?"

"Not so far," she grumbled. "He's willful." She'd bought a parenting book.

"I just thought, you know, you research everything. I figured you'd coach the same way. Articles and blogs and YouTube tutorials and wherever else you get your information."

She hadn't done that. He was right, that wasn't like her. She always made sure she was doing things correctly and efficiently and without cause for criticism. She now knew a great deal about being a turtle owner and about working at a nonprofit community center. Because she was a turtle owner and she did work at a nonprofit community center. But she hadn't devoted any of her time to properly learning how to be a youth basketball coach. "Huh."

"Not that I'm trying to…"

"No, you're right. I guess…I wasn't thinking like I am a coach. I didn't ever expect to be one. A lot has been happening that I didn't ever expect. I suppose I let this one get away from me a little."

"I hear that." Jay glanced over his shoulder and then looked back at her. "I never expected to run the community center."

"What? No way." She would've expected "I never expected to swim" from a fish before she'd hear those words from Jay Marler.

"No, I really didn't."

"You're good at it, though. How are you running it if you didn't intend to?"

"I don't think I ever didn't want to be the coordinator. I don't know. It's kind of what happened. My dad started it all up. Did I tell you that? You probably heard from somebody. So I basically grew up there. Worked a lot of summers there, helped out. I always liked it. Then my dad passed away, and I was already there, and it…you know. Here I am."

"Oh." She'd assumed the community center was Jay's baby. Like the B&B was to the Hayses. "But you like it, though. Right?"

He crossed his arms with a shrug. "Yeah. I like it."

She couldn't put her finger on it, but his words seemed shy of the whole truth. "Do you ever think about doing something different?"

"Nnnn—" He stopped and gave a measured, thinking-grimace. "I don't know. I pray about it sometimes." Jay straightened his back briefly and then leaned forward again, keeping his arms settled across his chest. He looked like he was trying to choose his words. Or maybe it was one of those things he was still trying to figure out. She could hear his heel drumming on the dirt under the picnic table. Like his body wasn't accustomed to being still so long.

Piper realized they hadn't done this much. The talking. At work or in the car, they shared quips and passing comments and instructions and work-related information. Always with something else to do. But this was different. The two of them engaged in conversation. With nothing else in particular to demand their attention. Sitting and talking. Like friends.

He let out a comfortable sigh and uncrossed his arms to lace his fingers together in front of him. "I don't know. I think God put me here. At SBCC. But I don't think He put me here forever. Or maybe He did." Jay shrugged with his eyebrows. "I don't know."

"What else are you passionate about?" She mentally prepared a spreadsheet.

"Me? I don't have time to be passionate about anything else."

"Aw, come on. You have to have something. Even just a hobby. Or an interest. Like I've got Hubcap. What about you? What's your turtle?"

"Isn't the turtle also, theoretically—or metaphorically maybe—the thing that wrecked your car and stranded you here in the first place?"

136

"Fair point."

"See, I generally try to avoid turtles where I can. Complicated...turtles." He flicked something she couldn't see off the bill of her hat. "I admire you, though. And your bedazzled turtle carrier."

Where did the sudden wave of shyness come from? Piper shook it off and answered, "It's not bedazzled. It's just a few tasteful, masculine rhinestones. And some of the sparkly Mod Podge." The carrier box had a galaxy theme now. So Hubcap was like a little astronaut. It was adorable.

She may have gone a hair overboard. Upon reflection.

"Yeah, okay. You're right, it's a completely reasonable thing to do." The half grin on his face made the sarcasm come across rather kind. "No, I'm just saying, it's good. Good for you. You had a turtle thrown at you pretty hard, and you leaned into it like no one I've ever known. Well handled, Piper Cope."

Her first response was the likely overblown feeling of blood rushing to her face because, compliments. But then what he actually said registered, and she realized how ridiculous he was. Well handled? What, in any of the time she'd known him, had she handled with any iota of grace whatsoever? She was currently sitting across from him looking like she lost a fight with a weed whacker, and once again sporting more dirt upon her person than she'd ever managed to collect at any point during her childhood, and they'd just established that she was failing pretty hard at coaching ten young boys in basketball fundamentals. And he didn't even know, he didn't know about Mark or her sister or how comprehensively bad she was at basic friendship with other humans. "I disagree."

"There's nothing I can do about that," he said, unbothered.

"But I appreciate it."

He made a cordial, you're welcome motion with one hand

"Wait," Piper said suspiciously. "How are we even talking about me right now? We were talking about you."

"Bon homies!" Kent appeared then, guitar in one hand, Kariss's hand in the other. "Hey, we have to go and pick up our small man child. We're getting ice cream after. Wanna come? Oh, nice hat, Pi. Wait, do I know that hat?" He leaned in to take a closer look. "Was that ever my hat?"

Jay answered, "Probably."

"Aw, awesome. I'm glad it went toward a good cause."

From any other person in the universe, Piper was sure that would've been insulting. But Kent looked sincerely glad. "Thank you."

"So? Ice cream? Yes? No?"

Piper looked at Jay to find him looking at her, asking the question with his eyebrows. Since he was her ride, if one went, they both had to go. He seemed content enough to let her make the call. "Sure."

"Sure." Jay agreed as he stood up. "Probably can't stay too late, though. I have to run by the center and do a few things. And there's church tomorrow."

Church tomorrow. "No." There it was. There was the horror. Descending upon her without mercy or reprieve. She didn't know how she'd forgotten tomorrow was Sunday. Today was Saturday, so tomorrow was Sunday. *Of course. Perfect.* She ran her hands down her face. Ouch. "Oh, why?"

"What?" Jay asked.

"Ugh, I can't get my hair cut before church tomorrow. My second time at this church, and I have to walk in looking like a four-year-old who tried cutting her own hair."

Kent piped up, "JJ cut my hair once. He did a pretty fantastic job, though, considering."

Kariss shook her head slowly beside him. Like No, that is incorrect. But then she said, "It was the best haircut he's ever had." So Piper wasn't sure what to make of it.

"On the bright side, though," Jay said, "maybe you'll be late and have to walk down the center aisle past every member of the seated congregation to the only available seat. Which will happen to be on the front row."

"I didn't even think of that! You don't understand. That could happen! I can't be late tomorrow." She pulled out her phone with the intent to set five different alarms for the morning. Then another thought occurred to her, and she looked up at Jay. "Wait, how is that the bright side?"

"You know. In case you're playing blackout rules in My Life's Actually a Sitcom BINGO." He was absolutely chewing the inside of his mouth. And it wasn't even all that effective.

"You appear to be enjoying this," she noted.

"I am trying very hard not to appear to be enjoying this."

She threw his hat at him, and part of her hitherto nonexistent bangs fell in her face.

CHAPTER FIFTEEN

❀

"You have reached the automatic voicemail box of…"

"Laurel Finch."

"After the tone…"

Piper hit "End Call" and pulled up her text message box. Stared for a moment at the little blinking cursor. "Enter message" it said. *Well,* she thought. I'm not sure exactly what my message is. So…is there an option for that? An emoji perhaps? How would that facial expression go? If they could draw it sort of shrugging maybe, open-mouthed with a question mark over its head like, *Uhhhhhh…?*

Her phone had one that was a plate of spaghetti. She could literally, with ease, text her sister an emoji plate of spaghetti. To be fair, that might be just as accurate a representation of her feelings as if she tried her hand at composing a text. Possibly more so. Laurel. I feel like a plate of spaghetti. Please advise. That seemed like an unhelpful thing to text someone.

She'd been in Silas Bend nearly four weeks now. Unbelievably enough. Any time she thought about it, she was caught in that paradoxical space between has-it-really-been-that-long and has-it-only-been-that-long. Four weeks. And every day that went by was a day closer to the end of her stay.

There had been a bit of phone tag between Piper and her sister. Sort of half-hearted phone tag if she was honest. More like phone hide-and-go-seek—where the seeker was mostly interested in peace and quiet, and the hider was just reading a book with a flashlight in the hall closet. They'd really done that. That was an actual part of Piper's childhood.

"How you doing in here, Starlet?" Shawley walked into the kitchen then, circumnavigating the island to pull a glass down from the cabinet.

Piper grinned and pushed up from where she'd been leaning against the counter next to the oven and straightened her borrowed, ruffly apron. Ever since Piper got her hair cut, Shawley had taken to calling her Starlet. She honestly didn't look anything like a starlet, but she thought it was interesting. She'd never had her hair this short. It stopped above her shoulders now, and there were bangs that angled down her forehead and fell just short of her eyes. Took some getting used to. But her head felt much lighter, and she no longer had to worry about things like snapped hair ties. "English matrimonials are officially in the oven," Piper reported. "They are officially baking. I am officially waiting."

"It all sounds terribly official." Shawley winked as she filled her glass with ice and water from the fridge's dispenser. "Those are some lucky little boys."

"I used a layer of chocolate chips instead of apricot jam. In compliance with their as yet unrefined palates." Boys.

"How considerate."

"I try not to make the same mistake twice." Apparently, in the opinion of about half her troupe, fruit filling was offensive unless in the form of a Pop-Tart. She couldn't be too put out. More for her. And Jay had liked them. Besides that, she felt a tad disappointed in herself for never having thought to make them with chocolate before. *Chocolate. It was so obvious.*

She moved to put oats and vanilla and flour and sugar and chocolate chips back in their appropriate places among the cheery, rustic wood cupboards and counter tops and the red brick back splash of Shawley's kitchen. Before Shawley Bea's, she'd never used a kitchen that had so many things. More appliances and cooking accoutrements than she knew what to do with. But it was satisfying to know they were there.

Shawley sipped at her ice water, pulling a stool out to sit at the island, leaning comfortably on an elbow. "Who you on the phone with?" she asked with a nod at the phone still in Piper's hand.

"Oh. No one. I was just going to call my sister. It went to voicemail. I'll get her later."

"The sister you're staying with when you leave here?"

"Presumably." Piper offered a smile.

"Everything all right there?" Shawley's face was open and kindly curious, her voice as frank as always. "You look glum, my dear."

"Oh, I don't think I'm glum. I think things are fine. I'm not…Laurel's been difficult to get a read on lately. For me. And when I left, things were a little… strained. Which was my fault, mainly. So. You know. It's awkward. Family things. It's not uncommon for those to be awkward, right?"

"How was it your fault?"

Piper shrugged. "I was an idiot." She paused and sent a jokingly beseeching look Shawley's way. "You don't want to raise an objection? Even just a small one? I thought we had a bond."

Shawley was equal parts good-humored and tactfully ruthless. "I wasn't there. Maybe you were an idiot."

"Definitely." Piper sighed. "I was engaged to be married. To a pastor. A future pastor anyway. And I think I acted…I guess I thought that made me somebody. Which is stupid, I know. I'm a hundred percent aware. I don't think I realized it so much then, but I left everyone behind so easily. Left Laurel behind like I'd outgrown her. Burned all these bridges because I was off to a new life." Shame and embarrassment collided in her stomach. She'd been so caught up in making her plans, moving forward in the life she was building for herself with her perfect man and her enlightened existence. "I'm afraid I behaved badly."

"Said some things, did you?"

"I really didn't. That's the thing. I didn't say much at all. I just packed up and left. Hardly a 'Sayonara, sucker,' called back over my shoulder. Off to live my own life with my own people."

Piper absently swiped the screen of her phone. Just to see something that wasn't a person with eyes that could read her soul, like Shawley. Did a quick check for notifications she knew weren't there. Her background image was of a sunset—though she couldn't swear it wasn't a sunrise—someone else had taken. Perfectly gorgeous pinks and purples and oranges descending into—or rising from?—a desert canyon somewhere she'd never been. *Wouldn't be difficult to make something up about it being symbolic for God's steadfastness or the way He made all things new.*

In reality, she'd been so hasty to replace the picture of Mark and her standing couple-close and smiling brightly that she'd slapped on the first unobjectionable image she came across. She didn't even remember choosing it. It was quite possible it had come with the phone.

"Honey," Shawley said, her tone both demanding Piper's attention and sympathizing entirely with her plight. There was something magical in the way Shawley said it, too. Piper had never been one of those people who could successfully call another person "Honey" without it sounding very forced and unnatural. When Shawley said it, it was warm and comforting and honest and made Piper relax a little. "Just for the record, I've done my share of offending other people, so you're not alone there. I've had to do my share of asking forgiveness for it too. Groveled through more than a slew of apologies to friends I've treated in a bad way. Way too many times to that husband of mine, I'm sad to tell you."

"What, you and Calvin?" Piper asked with a grin. "I thought you two were perfect."

"And I'm perfectly content you keep thinking that way. And tell your friends, too." She gave a short huff of a chuckle. "But there's some cockamamie rumor—we could call it reality, I suppose, if we have to—that we are in fact just regular, sin-abounding people. Can you even imagine." Her face still held her usual humor, but her gaze turned weightier as she looked at Piper.

"'Bout every time I've behaved badly like that it's been a result of my own foolish pride. I can think of more than one time, too, when I was too blame stubborn to humble myself without the Lord prompting me. And by 'prompting' I mean He's got to haul me off the top of my silly ol' high horse. Usually in a most undignified way. My high horses tend to be terribly tall. Miles. Miles and miles tall."

"Undignified like getting dumped by your fiancé and then running into a tree to avoid a turtle?" Piper

146

offered. It even stung to say the first part. Even now. Unreasonably so.

"Aww, now. Who doesn't tell that story?"

Piper felt her lips quirk up at that. She took a step closer to the island, leaning over on both elbows across from Shawley.

The woman across from her took another swallow of water before saying, in a tone Piper would call the vocal equivalent of business casual, "So I'll say, from one idiot to another, I've been through all that enough times to know that if your pride made you too big for your skinny little I'm-gonna-be-a-pastor's-wife britches, you might've been something of an idiot. But even so, though, I can't doubt for a minute that your sister loves you and would want to mend any fences."

A small seed of hope sprouted deep within Piper. It would need watering. Piper was better with turtles than plants.

"Maybe that's just me sitting where I am and not knowing all the situation," Shawley said, "but even if she's not, it's good to make sure we've done everything we can on our end to make our relationships right, isn't it? I'll just say it is. The Bible says so, so I can say so. 'If it's possible, so far as it depends on you, live at peace with everyone.' That's right in Romans, right there to read. Maybe she won't ever want to be close with you again. But I figure, 'as far as it depends on you' means sometimes you gotta get humble and make an effort at fixing whatever you've wronged."

If the woman didn't speak truth, Piper might have fought to change the subject.

"I don't know about you," Shawley said, not waiting for a response, "but for me, humility hasn't been a quick and easy lesson to learn. I'm always having to learn it and re-learn it. And then, by golly, learn it again. Maybe that's why the Lord teaches it from so many directions in the Word. Jesus, of course, being the perfect example of being God and then giving up all His rights as God and humbling Himself all the way to that cross. I'll never stop being amazed by that. Our salvation is a direct result of His humility. That moves me, inspires me, and convicts me all at once."

Piper knew the cross part. *How much time had she spent considering the "humbled Himself" part?*

"But even just last week I noticed I'd gotten all cocky about something petty." Shawley popped the table a solid smack with her palm and straightened on her stool, leaning away from the counter top. "Good night a-livin'," she harrumphed, "it was like the rooster thinking the sun comes up just to hear his crow. Well, that very morning, lo and behold, the Lord landed me smack-dab in the first two chapters of the book of Ruth in my Bible-reading plan. Knock me down and steal my teeth!"

Knock me down and steal my teeth. What? Southern charm is weird. Hilariously, beautifully inelegant. "Those aren't your real teeth?" Piper teased.

"Oh, you just hush. I'm telling you about Ruth."

"I'm sorry, tell me about Ruth."

Shawley had a crooked, knowing set to her face. She jutted her jaw to one side and tilt her head forward so she could look directly over her glasses. "Ruth experienced loss. Lost her young husband. Lost her own people, her culture, her home, her security, and her future."

Piper had done a whole study on Ruth during her pastor's-wife-in-training days, and she hadn't thought about relating to the woman so much.

Shawley went on. "But she humbled herself to accept as her own a God her people didn't know. She was humble when she committed herself to her mother-in-law and to her needs. She gleaned in a field like her mother-in-law said to, and you know, that was considered a lowly thing. Humility. I just kept seeing more places where Ruth modeled it. And the Lord didn't let me go even at that. It was like everywhere I read in the Good Book the next couple of days, I was confronted again with another lesson in humility."

The older woman chuckled, and it was softer and sweeter than usually she chuckled. "God is always faithful to keep a lesson coming whether I'm too mule-headed to receive it or not. Sometimes it happens when I open up His Word, like it was last week. Or sometimes it's when I'm praying. I'll be praying along and, boom! There's my big, fat, ugly pride right in my face. Lord-a-mercy. It's uglier than homemade soap."

Piper waited for her to add her personal south-ernism favorite—uglier than homemade sin. Shawley barreled ahead.

"But the Lord is always right there with His grace, too—ready and waiting for the asking. And big enough to cover it all. Big enough to give me the strength to ask for forgiveness. Or to humbly serve when I don't want to. Or to give up what I want so someone else can have what they need. Or to stop being such a Pharisee. Or...to tell somebody I've been an idiot."

Piper watched Shawley's fingers idly play across the counter top. "Humble pie is never going to taste like gingerbread," Shawley said, "but it sets life back in order, sort of getting our soul lined up with the humble soul of Jesus. So I reckon I'll keep on having another slice."

Piper mimicked the pattern Shawley had drawn with her own fingers. "I'm not sure I've humbled myself with my sister. I don't want to have to admit to her—or to me—that I'm as awful as I am."

"On our own, we're all pretty awful, darling. You're not done yet. You don't make allowances for that, like it's an excuse. But it's hope, though. That God's still working on you."

"I think maybe it'll be good in a way," Piper said, and for the second time, felt a little seed of belief and hope as she said it, "staying with her when I leave. Assuming the offer is still on the table. Maybe I can try to repair some things." What would it be like, living there, though? What if it made things worse? "I just can't say I'm really looking forward to it. So, if you're running low on prayer requests…"

"Consider yourself prayed for," Shawley said.

"Thank you."

Shawley shimmied herself off the stool, and checked the matrimonials in the oven. "Mmhm. Well. That was a lovely talk. Wasn't expecting that." She spoke mostly into the oven when she said, "I'd figured you'd be on the phone with someone else."

"Why?"

The woman hummed innocently. "Thought it was a certain young man I know who seems to text you quite a lot."

Piper groaned. "Shawley, no."

❁

Jay walked into the gym with one goal in mind: cookies. Oatmeal cookie and a layer of chocolate chips. Thick and square and up until this point remarkably well-guarded. Piper had entered that morning in her basketball shorts and t-shirt. The moment she'd seen him, she'd turned halfway and curled her shoulders over to protect the foil-wrapped plate in her hands. "No," she'd said. "These are for my team. Stop looking like that. Don't even think about it."

Which wasn't fair because he hadn't even noticed the plate before she said something. "What are they?"

"English matrimonials."

"They don't even like those."

"They're chocolate this time." He must've made some kind of interested face because her eyes narrowed into a glare. "No."

Then she'd hidden them. Not that he'd gone looking. Who had that kind of time? But they definitely hadn't been in the fridge or the office or underneath the bleachers.

Now it was nearing the end of her practice, and he stayed by the door for a minute, watching as Piper ran her team through a layup drill, the players forming two lines so each one could practice shooting from both the left and right side of the hoop. She stood at the end line, under the basket, a whistle hanging around her neck. Looking for all the world like she might accidentally be having a good time coaching basketball.

"Pass it from your chest, Arthur. Yep, just like that. Nice. Nice basket, Noah. There…Wayne, don't tickle your teammate. There's no tickling in basketball. There is only…playing basketball. Nice shot, though."

She shifted her weight from heel to heel as she watched her team, focused on her players, putting forth a thousand times more confidence than she had that first night. It lacked the entertainment value of her first go-around, but made up for it in the way it was…it was nice. She looked pleased with where she was, and he liked how it looked on her.

Piper glanced up and spotted him, immediately turning to glare at him sideways, wary and suspicious.

Her eyes shot a quick look toward the bleachers. Aha. He followed her gaze. The forbidden plate.

"Keep it up, guys," she said and made her way toward him, approaching at an angle in a way that he almost would have called sneaky if they hadn't been looking at each other. "Whatcha doing, Marler?" she asked, the offhand words losing any offhandedness to her low, guarded voice.

"Cope," he greeted in the same dramatic tone, eyeballing her right back. "You know why I'm here. What is that kid doing?" One of the kids had his phone out and appeared to be taking video of the other players as they did their layups and passed the ball back to the line.

"Hm? Oh, Finn. Yeah, he hates basketball." She sounded perfectly cheery about that, cheery enough to forget they were supposed to be having a mildly cool battle of wills over cookies to which Jay had no legal claim. "But he's super into making videos. So we made a deal that if he runs around basketballing for the first half of practice, I let him shoot footage for the highlight reel he's working on. I've seen some of his work. For an eleven-year-old, he is exceptional. Basically I want to keep him forever."

Step by step they neared the bleachers.

"Oh, hey, Tony—the Jasper twins' dad—said at the end of season he'd like to host a little get-together barbecue for the team. So we're going to let Finn have his film-making career debut, and the kids'll all get to see themselves and how they've improved. And apparently

Tony has some sort of secret family recipe for three-bean casserole, which initially I wasn't very excited about, honestly. But I have been told by multiple people that it is so worth it."

He grinned at her grin. He couldn't help it. "I will go ahead and confirm the rumors. Tony Jasper makes three-bean casserole exciting. I don't know what he does, but it is basically dessert." And there. There was the perfect segue. "Speaking of desserts…" he said smoothly. Nailed it.

She checked her cookie hoard conspicuously before raising her whistle to her lips and giving two short, shrill blasts. "Boys!" she called, loud enough to gather the attention of all of her company. "Jay Marler over here has an eye for the baked goods previously ear-marked for team members only. Thoughts?"

There were a few looks of easy assent, but before any of them could really become vocal, Noah, true to form, called, "No way! Those are for us." But he was beaming and being a snarky little rabble-rouser more than having any real objections. Some of the other boys snickered along with him and agreed firmly with his initial response of "No way."

"Aw, come on, guys," he tried appealing to any sense of pity they might have.

"Nope," Noah maintained, and some of his buddies crossed their arms, all of them clearly enjoying wielding their terrible power. "Not happening."

Piper looked amused enough in her own right. "Well, I guess they've spoken. They did work very hard today in practice. I did promise them matrimonials." She always called them that. They were cookie bars.

"And you—you, Piper Cope—didn't make any extras?" Impossible.

She only said, "Hmmm…" As though she was pondering. As though it was not a yes or no question.

Then Jay got a brilliant idea. "Okay, what about this, hard workers," he addressed the boys, only glancing periodically at their coach. "How about," he said slowly, "I put some work in. It's only fair. How about we play some Knockout. If I win, and I beat all ten of you, I get two cookies. If I lose…I…only get one."

Finn held up one quizzical finger, but the rest of the guys were already bouncing and cheering for Knockout.

He played Knockout with his team all the time. He could definitely take on ten fifth and sixth graders. He tried to put as much swagger into the look he sent in Piper's direction as he could. She smirked back at him. "I'll even shoot first. Like Han in the cantina."

There were cheers once again as the boys surged forward to line up behind Jay at the free throw line. Noah was behind him with a ball—of course he was—showing his teeth like a shark.

"Does everybody know how to play Knockout?" he asked diplomatically. Less diplomatically he asked, "Does everybody know how to lose at Knockout?" which made them groan and promise he'd be the one to lose until he called their attention again. "Okay. Two balls.

First guy shoots from the free throw line. If you make it, you pass the ball to the next guy and go to the end of the line. If you miss, you pick up your rebound, and you shoot again from anywhere in front of the free throw line until you make it in. After your first shot, whether you make it or not, the person behind you is gonna shoot. If he makes his shot before you make yours, you're out. Last man standing—i.e. me—wins. Eats cookies. That is Knockout. Any questions?"

They were ready to play. Jay shot his ball, made it the first time for his first couple of turns. The line quickly diminished in the way of all Knockout lines, amid shouting and cheering and cries of defeat.

With only three boys left, Jay felt pretty good. He shot again, and the ball bounced off the rim, but he'd picked it up and dropped it neatly in the basket before Noah could even get a shot off behind him. Made it look easy. He glanced at Piper, bouncing his eyebrows with enough put-on cockiness to telegraph, *The cookies shall be mine*, and tossed the ball to Chase, behind Noah. As he was jogging back, though, Noah ran forward to retrieve his own ball, and Jay had to course correct mid-stride.

Oh no. His left ankle rolled at just the wrong angle as his weight came down. More surprising than painful. And then he was falling.

It didn't feel like a graceful fall. Didn't especially feel like a dignified, athletic, manly sort of dive either. Felt like the sort of thing that would happen in eighth grade gym class in front of the girls. Like he suddenly had too many gangly limbs, and they all tangled in that moment to land him sprawled like an awkward pile of beach-bound octopus. Like an awkward pile of beach-bound octopus in its eighth grade gym class.

He pushed himself up to a sitting position, feeling heat rush to his face. Piper's team had formed a half circle around him. Some of them were fighting laughter. Some of them were not fighting hard enough. "Well. Ouch."

"Are you all right?" Piper asked. She was one of the onlookers losing the battle.

His ankle was sore. A sharp, uncomfortable, too-warm sort of pain suggested some torn blood vessels. "Turned my ankle the wrong way."

Her amusement evaporated in an instant. "Oh, seriously? Are you okay?"

"Ah, yes. Yes. I think I'm…embarrassed." Really that qualified as okay, because things that were merely embarrassing were generally funny. Right?

"Oh my gosh, you can have all the cookies."

That received immediate protests from the boys. But Piper seemed to be going into disaster mode.

"Can you stand? Maybe you should stay still. Should I call…? Do you need an ambulance? You're supposed to get a frozen bag of peas to stop the swelling. I don't have a bag of peas. I've got no peas, Jay!"

"There are ice packs in the short freezer, though," he pointed out calmly.

"It's not supposed to be an ice pack, it's supposed to be peas! Do you know nothing about first aid?"

"You're a really great person to have around in an emergency. Do you know that?"

It was hardly an issue to get up and limp over to the bleachers. He sat with his foot elevated and ice-compressed, eating cookies and chatting with kids' parents as they came by to retrieve them. Piper eventually sat next to him.

"How is it?"

"It's fine. Probably be sore for a couple days. I think it'll be more annoying than anything else."

"Did you do this to make me feel better about all the black eyes and getting my head stuck to a bike and stuff?"

"Of course I did."

Her smile stretched into something wide that crinkled the edges of her eyes, and suddenly there was a little brown birthmark above her right eyebrow, hardly bigger than a freckle. It must've always been there, but he noticed it now.

"And you didn't throw the game on purpose to get pity matrimonials?" She went on like she didn't even know about her interesting birthmark.

"Pity cookies taste every bit as good as victory cookies."

"Ugh. Never give an inspirational speech. And you really can't call them matrimonials, can you."

"I really can't."

"Fine." She clapped her hands on her thighs and stood up. "I'm going to start herding people to the doors and locking this place down."

"Appreciate it."

She eyeballed him instead of moving away. "Are you okay to drive tonight?"

"I've only had Tylenol, Piper."

"Hm." She considered him and his ankle for a moment. "Want me to get the two-wheel hand truck thing and roll you out to your car as fast as I can?"

"Yes." There was no way this would end well, and he couldn't wait.

CHAPTER SIXTEEN

❀

The mid-June sun beat down with predictable relentlessness. Piper could feel it beginning to sizzle at the tops of her shoulders and, in doing so, providing illumination for her 20/20 hindsight that sunblock would've been a really intelligent idea.

There hadn't been much room for intelligence in her preparations, however. Most of her intelligence had been stowed in corners and under furniture and into the dustiest attics and garages of her mind in order to make absolutely certain there was enough room for all the shock. She'd gotten the text from Kariss the night before.

<<You want to go to the flea market with me tomorrow after your basketball game?

Kariss.

Kariss Peeper. Had wanted to go out flea marketing. With her. Just the two of them. It was no time for intelligent thinking. It was a time for worrying Calvin at the kitchen table with her various, floundering shock-noises and for not questioning why she couldn't get the *Twilight Zone* theme out of her head.

But now she walked side by side with Kariss Peeper, shooting glances at the other woman often enough that she'd yet to become aware of what sort of junk vendors were pushing from the network of tables they passed.

This is cool. This is a cool…thing. She liked Kariss. She'd seen her around a bunch of times. But it hadn't occurred to her that Kariss would be the type to go flea market shopping on a Saturday afternoon. And it certainly hadn't occurred to her that she would be the type to want company. At least not Piper's company. Because *She is like a thousand degrees cooler than me!*

Piper finally managed to look around as Kariss stopped to dig through a large plastic tote of old action figures at the base of a table that seemed mainly devoted to a pre-2005 collection of DVDs and VHS tapes. Impressive selection. Could've used a better inventory system. The vendor was a pleasant-faced, middle-aged man sitting in a lawn chair a few feet away with a battery-operated fan and a cigarette, looking like he'd been doing this for years. He smiled at her. She returned it and waved.

So this was a flea market. She'd never been to one before. It wasn't incredibly large or overwhelming, she estimated around 30 or 40 collapsible tables set up in haphazard groupings across a motel parking lot. They were far enough away from the highway that she couldn't hear traffic sounds, and the atmosphere was dusty and slapdash but friendly enough. The early-summer humidity wasn't so high as to make everyone miserable, but it did make the hot air seem closer and as if she were wearing an imaginary extra layer over her tank top.

Kariss picked out two toys from the bin and held them up, one in each hand. "Opinion?"

One of them looked like some sort of transformer, but off brand. The other was a space vehicle in the style of late 80s cartoons. "Who is it for?" The easy guess was JJ. But then there was also Kent, and Piper would not have been surprised if the toy was for him.

"JJ."

"Oh, yeah, it's his birthday soon, isn't it. Hm, well? I like the ship. And I think it seems sturdier."

Kariss considered for a moment. Then she nodded and paid the man before stowing the toy in the oversize tote bag on her shoulder.

Quite a few people milled about among the tables. Some of the displays were impressive. Hand-made art pieces or well-preserved antiques with suitably hefty price tags. Other tables were cluttered with post-garage sale castoffs. Fifteen-year-old jeans and shadeless lamps and stuffed animals poignantly but irreparably contaminated by love.

Piper stopped at a massive collection of empty glass soda bottles. "I never got the whole old soda bottle thing. Every thrift store has old soda bottles. What do you do with them? Should you carry one around in case you get stranded on a deserted island and you need to get a message out?" She turned the corners of her mouth down. "I wouldn't use a bottle. I would train a sea gull. I would wrangle it and then train it."

She looked over to see Kariss giving her an exclamatory eyebrow.

"What?" Piper asked. "There's at least as good a chance of that working as there is someone finding your bottled message within your lifetime. Don't look at me like that. What would you do?"

Kariss didn't even hesitate. "Survive."

Piper could easily see Kariss with a homemade spear and a knife fashioned from the bones of a giant, man-eating fish she'd had to slay with her own hands. "Remind me to invite you to my desert island stranding."

She could have sworn there was something of a smile there.

They browsed a few minutes, walking in and out of the jumbled rows of booths. At one point they came upon several bicycles leaning threateningly on their kickstands. Piper gave those vicious devils wide berth, resisting the urge to reach up to protect what was left of her hair. She pointedly ignored Kariss and her smirk.

At least three or four times a day, Piper still instinctively reached for the ponytail holder that once had a perpetual home around her left wrist. Even if her new hairstyle was—oh, she wasn't even going to think the phrase *growing on her*—she maintained her right to hold a grudge on inanimate objects. It wasn't a phobia. It was a principle. Hey, it was practically political. Bicycles were aggressively anti-hair and couldn't be reasoned with, and Piper was not fully prepared to encounter one amicably in a social setting.

She couldn't help but notice that both of them picked up their pace as they passed a collection of brightly dressed and painted ceramic clowns. She shared a look of deep understanding with her flea market mate. The little frozen-eyed figurines were probably there because they'd murdered their previous owner. The creepy baby doll in Piper's room at Shawley Bea's suddenly seemed downright genial in comparison, and she felt she might owe it an apology.

They stopped and took their time at a table with stacks and stacks of books. Old books, new books, slightly water-damaged books, recognizable bestsellers, and obscure, likely out-of-print titles with incomprehensible cover art. All the books.

"Ooh, hey!" Piper pulled out a yellow, hardcover children's book about dinosaurs in the Bible. "JJ doesn't have this, does he? Would he like it if I got it for his birthday?"

Kariss glanced up and gave an approving, "Definitely." Kariss found a couple of paperbacks she said she'd read in elementary school and a mystery novel neither of them had ever heard of.

Piper tucked her purchase under one arm and got distracted by an elderly woman selling preserves out of the back of her minivan. She picked up a jar of blackberry jam for Calvin and Shawley. Then she got distracted again by what might have been a black market transaction of an illegal lawn dart set between a couple of friendly gents a few yards away. The people around here were really hardcore about their leisurely recreational activities.

By the time she was less distracted, Kariss had her hands on a replica of one of those old, candlestick telephones, eyeballing it sternly.

"Hey, cool. You gonna ask Sarah to ring up Aunt Bea for you?" she joked.

Kariss hummed. "Kent collects telephones."

"Kent collects telephones? Why?"

"Because they make him happy."

"Well, that's not fair. What doesn't make Kent happy?"

It earned an eyebrow-raise/head-tilt combo of point acknowledgment. "He just likes phones. He says some of his favorite memories are phone conversations with friends." She paused. "There's a framed poster of Alexander Graham Bell in the den."

"Where did you get a poster of Alexander Graham Bell?"

"It's actually a poster of the third-season cast of *Saved By the Bell*, but he put a printout of Alexander Graham Bell's face over each of their faces."

Piper almost spit, "What does that even mean?"

"He has a complicated mind."

Piper laughed out loud. *How did Kariss carry on this kind of conversation with a straight face?* "So how many does he have? In his collection I mean."

"This one will make sixty-four I think."

"Hold the phone," she said.

At that, Kariss burst out in genuine laughter. Who knew Kariss could do that? And at something so *lame*. Piper couldn't help but laugh along. She'd expected a nice day, but this was fun. She was having fun with Kariss Peeper.

Piper stumbled upon a treasure of a coffee mug. Chunky ceramic with a wide base and narrower top. A mug meant to hold serious levels of hot beverage, but comfortable to wrap her hands around. Darkish maroon—not very summery, but she could say it was the color of raspberry jam. An easy and exciting buy. She immediately dubbed it her new favorite thing.

The next item she came across was a single, high-backed kitchen chair with which she fell irrevocably in love for no reason at all. It was kind of a pitiful old bear. Looked like it had been some little girl's art project once upon a time. Aged but sturdy wood. Even though it was dirty and the paint was cracked, Piper could see the wide, clumsy brushstrokes. The legs, seat, and back were mismatched colors: green and blue and pink and red and yellow. Indecipherable shapes and swirls, obviously painted by someone with no appreciation for a color wheel. It was a train wreck. But she found it inexplicably, inexpressibly charming.

She couldn't buy it. *Of course not.* Regardless of the price, what would she do with a chair? This really wasn't the time in her life to start collecting furniture, even if she could think of a hundred fun ways to use this pleasant, ugly thing. For a brief moment, she did wish she had a house to put…under and around it. And wasn't that an odd shuffle of priorities? *Wish my life were more stable so I could buy this chair.*

She found it interesting though, that her first instinct was not a longing to have a home. More to the point, her knee-jerk reaction was not a longing to have a home with Mark. The home she'd expected. Shouldn't there have been a pang of loss, like there had been before? It had all seemed so close. When she thought of a someday-home, it was supposed to have him in it. Him and their children and their life. When she thought about bringing a chair into her home, she should be considering whether or not he'd like it. She didn't know if he'd have liked the chair, honestly. He could've loved it or hated it; she had no idea. But it didn't matter. It didn't matter because she was thinking of a future and a home, and it wasn't poisoned by the Mark-fog that had made looking forward such a daunting and painful concept.

"Are you going to get that chair?" Kariss's low voice sounded beside her, and Piper realized with a start that Kariss stared at the chair along with her.

"What? No. Shh. I think I'm having a break-through."

Kariss nodded like that wasn't completely weird and went back to staring. She did lean her head to the side, regarding the chair with perhaps more intensity than she had been.

It really was just an ugly chair. But it also felt oddly like…she was healing. *Things were getting better.*

Lord, thank you for this ugly chair. And Kariss and all the weird, really weird, ways You've been getting my attention lately. I really want to know what You're doing. What I'm supposed to be doing. But thank You for this piece of…peace. Right now. You snuck it right up on me.

She would someday like to have a home and a family. That was still her heart's desire. But it was okay that it wasn't right now. And that it wasn't with Mark. More than okay.

Piper turned away from the chair. "Breakthrough over. Shall we? After this, do you want to grab an early dinner?"

Kariss agreed. They spent another forty minutes walking around. Piper managed to get a selfie of the two of them looking terrified in front of the clown table. Well, Piper looked terrified. Kariss looked like a good sport.

On their way to Kariss's SUV, Piper found a painting she thought would look all right on the blank wall over Jay's couch in his office. It was cheap. She picked it up without debating too much on whether it was a good idea.

They drove back into town and stopped at Olive's Café on Main Street. Piper had been in before to grab a sandwich on her way somewhere a few weeks ago. It was nice to go in and sit down. The place was small but clean and decorated like a trendy coffee shop. Burnt orange walls and dark brown accents. Cushioned booths and benches. Apparently the interior had been recently overhauled. Piper hadn't seen it before the renovation, but she loved how it had turned out.

Piper ordered a chicken salad sandwich and Kariss a salad with breaded chicken and cranberries and a plate of fried jalapeños.

As soon as they sat down, before they even got their food, Kariss asked, point blank, "So what was the breakthrough?"

It surprised Piper. She would've bet on Kariss not asking. But Kariss sat across from her, expecting an answer. Piper didn't have to tell her. But she really wanted to. "I was engaged to a guy. Did I tell you that?" It was a silly, reflexive question. Of course Piper hadn't told her.

Kariss didn't look shocked. But it would've been startling to see her shocked about anything. "No."

"Mark. We'd been dating, or 'officially dating' for two years. We broke up a few weeks before I came to Silas Bend. I should have expected it. Probably. But I didn't."

"Oh." Kariss laid her hands calmly on the table. "Are you doing okay now?"

It was strange to have Kariss looking at her so directly, gaze relentless but with an unpredicted, honest quality about it. It was nice of her to ask. Piper didn't think Kariss would have asked unless she really wanted to know. "I am. Actually. I haven't been so much. But I'm getting there."

"Good. Why'd you break up?"

"Oh, you know. He gave a lot of reasons. But I don't think any of them were really the reason. Or at least…I think he was right. Now. Not necessarily about his reasons, but about us not being a good idea. Which is weird. It's so weird to think about because—what? Like two months ago? Just over?—I was prepared to marry this guy. Do the 'rest of our lives' bit. And now I look back, and it's like…I don't miss him. I mean, I do. He was a big part of my life, and there were things about it that were so nice. But the thing is, I don't know that I was even in love with him. Not the way you need to love someone you're going to marry. I think I was just really in love with my plan. He was great in a lot of ways, but mostly he was…convenient. How horrible does that sound? Like he fit my list. You know?"

Kariss took a sip of her tea. "Never had a list. Didn't think I'd need one."

"Why?"

"I was really odd as a kid." Kariss smirked. It was a great smirk. "Besides, if I'd made a list then, I'm pretty sure it wouldn't have looked anything like Kent."

Piper laughed out loud. "Good point."

"People say we don't make any sense. But he's my whole list now. And anyway, I've never been one for having plans. Me and Kent almost never have plans. I love it." Her face was softer when she spoke about him.

170

And it was a credit to them both that her expression looked less molded than it usually did. More inadvertent. Effortless.

"You beautiful, stoic, lover of life."

The words didn't faze Kariss. "I am all of those things," she agreed. With deadpan poise. "Yes."

Their food came then. After thanking the waitress, Kariss surprised Piper yet again by volunteering to pray for their meal. Her prayer was short and simple and sweet. And she thanked God for a Saturday afternoon out with a friend. *That's what they were.*

When she'd finished, after they'd started in on their food, Kariss pushed the as yet untouched plate of jalapeños toward Piper. "You can eat those."

"Not a fan of the peppers, amiga. Thanks, though."

Kariss tossed her salad around with her fork. "Well, I'm not eating them."

"Well, I'm not eating them. Why'd you order them if you don't want to eat them?"

"For the story."

"What story?"

"'Peeper and Piper picked at a plate of pepper poppers.'"

Piper dropped her sandwich and nearly stood up on the spot. She managed to point and sputter-shout,

"You-and-Kent. It does make sense! It makes sense right now!"

Then the smirk.

Piper sunk to her chin in the hallway bathroom's tub and pretended to be a turtle. She'd run the water cooler than she'd usually like, and it felt like a heavenly blessing on her sunburned shoulders. By the time she and Kariss parted ways, Piper had a lovely case of weekend fatigue and a not-so-lovely case of post-flea-market ripeness. After delivering the blackberry jam to Calvin and convincing him he really did not want to hug her just yet, she'd slipped upstairs and into the bath, thoroughly content and smiling.

How long had it been since she'd had a day like this? Just a day out with a girlfriend? Wow, how long had it been since she'd had a girlfriend? She'd allowed her free time—and most points in her life really—to be wrapped up in all things Mark. In his schooling and ministry and ambitions and him. When she'd been with other people, it was usually with him, as a couple. Not that it was his fault. That was on her. But right now, on a day when she'd unwisely agreed to a contest of who could hold more fried jalapeños in her mouth without flinching—like she'd ever beat Kariss in a straight face competition—she remembered just how much she'd missed having a bud.

CHAPTER SEVENTEEN

❀

An entire aisle of snack crackers. Club crackers and pretzel crackers and round crackers and cracker chips. While Piper was sure the visiting youth drama team wouldn't want their cheese tray full of something as pedestrian as saltines, beyond that point she was entirely ignorant of proper cracker etiquette. She glanced down at her grocery list, as though she expected the answer to be there, even though—as the person who'd written the list—she was all too aware that after crackers the only available hint was a parenthetical for cheese tray.

Piper's phone buzzed in her pocket.

Jay Marler:

>>Marco

Amusement cut a warm, unexpected line through her internal cracker debate so suddenly she scrunched up her face for no one's benefit but her own and quickly shot back,

Me:

<<Polo?

She bit her lower lip and waited. Only a few seconds went by before her phone buzzed and lit up in her hand. She read,

Jay Marler:

>>I have realized my mistake.

Ah, yes. An inaudible game of Marco Polo is an ineffective way to locate someone.

Jay Marler:

>>Where are you?

Me:

<<Cracker aisle.

Piper checked her list. If he'd grabbed a needle for the bicycle pump—which seemed likely as that was his mission—they'd be done as soon as the cracker debate settled itself. The first time they'd gone shopping together for SBCC supplies, there had been no list. Jay was the "I'll remember what we need" type, which translated into the "I'll make several educated guesses about what we need" type, which meant they'd spent a good deal of time taking extra laps to make sure they weren't forgetting anything. Piper was a different type. She had a list with quantities pre-figured and items arranged in sequence of store layout, and she was more than a little proud supply runs now took half the time.

Even if, perhaps, extra time out with Jay wouldn't have been the worst thing in the world.

"Marco," Jay announced as he turned up the aisle toward her.

"Polo," she replied automatically.

"Oh, good. It worked. I found you." He tossed the bike pump needle into the cart among packs of disposable table cloths and frozen pizzas and a toilet plunger to replace the one Piper had hurled into the dumpster in a fit of post-traumatic stress following a taco night. "We ready to go?"

"Almost. Close your eyes and spin around eleven times. We'll just buy whatever kind of crackers you dizzily stumble into."

"What if I knock over a shelf? Or another person?" Not *But why?* Rather, a debate over the logistics of the thing.

"Jay," she admonished. "Cracker choosing always involves some risk."

He heaved a heavy sigh. He closed his eyes. And he started spinning. With his face settled into a somewhat grim but ultimately comfortable expression of inevitability, he turned in place, mumbling "One..." under his breath and continuing to count for each rotation. He did pause—in his counting, not his spinning—to ask "Why eleven times?"

175

"You ask entirely the wrong questions. That's eight…nine…"

At eleven, he opened his eyes facing the wrong side of the aisle and had to turn around to clumsily punch the first box of crackers he could reach, knocking it over and sending another box to the floor.

"Why did you punch them?" Piper asked, finally dissolving into helpless laughter.

"Why was I spinning?" But he was laughing, too, and had to hold onto a lower shelf for balance as he bent down to retrieve a fallen package of buttery rounds.

Piper grabbed the dented box of wheat some-things where it had toppled off the shelf and held them up. "You may question my methods on a day when they're not an unmitigated success." In point of fact, she hadn't expected him to spin.

"We're going to pretend that most of the crackers in that box aren't broken?"

"Yes." Which seemed fair, considering he was the one who punched the box.

Supply runs were so much more efficient when she was around.

On the drive back to the community center, Jay and Piper spotted Kent coming out of the bakery at the town square. The man hopped up onto the base of the statue in the square's well-manicured center, arm slung over the statue's formally-postured shoulders for balance, and waved his white, bakery box of hopefully-not-something-fragile-or-frosted at them until Jay pulled his car into a parking space. For a moment, Piper enjoyed the incongruity of the gray, static, hard-line features of the statue and Kent's always-animated accidental irreverence.

"Hey, hey, hey, hey!" Kent called as he hopped down and ran over to them while Jay rolled down his window. "Dude! I was gonna text you! Now I don't have to text you!" Then he smiled big and said, "Hi, Piper."

"Text me what?" Jay asked.

"About whether you're still coming to dinner tonight. Are you still coming to dinner tonight?"

Jay did that slow inhale through rounded lips, head tilting back, wide-eyed expression he did that looked like the dawn and usually meant he'd just remembered something he'd forgotten. "Yes. Definitely yes."

"Excellent. Yeah, Kariss is making something sweet. Well, metaphorically sweet. Maybe literally sweet. I honestly don't know what she's making, but it will be amazing because she is amazing. Oh, and I got these pastries, and Piper, you have to come, too!" Kent looked at her with his own louder version of the dawn face. "If you can, you should definitely come. JJ will want to read his dinosaur book to you. Well, not read per se. But he knows all his letters now. He does have a hard time with the letter c. Which, you know, when it comes down to it, so do I. Like sometimes it makes a 'suh' sound, and sometimes it makes a 'kuh' sound, and both of those sounds you can already make with other letters. C, what is the point of having you at all?"

"Well, c is for cookie," Piper pointed out.

"And that's good enough for me," Jay finished, straight faced.

Kent looked back and forth between them. "What are you talking about? Piper, you're coming right?"

Piper went through some on-the-spot stalling. "I…wuh…ee… If Kariss was planning for…"

"Kariss thinks you're bees' knees. All the bees. With all their knees. And she always makes plenty of whatever she makes, and anyway, I can text her so she'll know."

Piper glanced at Jay. He advised, "You should probably say yes."

"Yes. Thanks. Sounds like fun."

"Whoop!" He smacked Jay's door in celebration. "Okay. Six o'clock then. I'll see you two later. My truck is parked on the other side of the statue."

"Who is that statue supposed to be anyway?" She'd been by it several times but kept forgetting to read the inscription on the plinth.

Kent stuck his head all the way inside the car to talk to her so Jay had to lean back in his seat and roll his eyes at the ceiling. "That's Silas Bend! He founded our town."

"'Silas Bend' is the name of a guy?"

Jay pushed Kent out by his face to cut in flatly, "His name was John Silas, and you have got to stop telling people that."

"Right!" Kent came back brightly. "Okay, well. Six o'clock. At mine. Double date. Well, double date plus my child son. I love it."

Jay glanced at her as Kent skipped off. Smiled a shruggy, helpless sort of smile. Neither of them mentioned the phrase double date because it obviously wasn't a double date. It was just Kent being loose with his terminology. So when she let out a nervous laugh she hadn't realized was building within her, it was likely unrelated. And anyway, Jay didn't seem to notice.

Jay,

You are allowed to hate this. But it was at the flea market for a steal, and I thought, "Hey, this might look all right over the couch in Jay's office." More honestly I thought, "Being in Jay's office is like being in a particularly roomy coffin if coffins had bowls of nasty stale candy." Thought you might like the brightening. Hang it if you want it. Don't if you don't. In any case, happy Friday.

Piper

Alone sitting on the green couch in his office, Jay could pretend he wasn't smiling goofily at the note. He'd gotten to see a bit more of his office since Piper settled in. She acted as a lovely buffer. Instead of getting calls every second, they'd tapered off to every other second, and he'd gotten to catch his breath. It was nice. The note taped to the painting was nicer.

He thought back to last night's dinner with Kent and Kariss and cringed inwardly. He may have cringed outwardly, but if so, that was the nice thing about his office coffin's walls—no one to see.

It had started out well enough. Kent came into the sitting room with a dish announcing he'd made the appetizer himself. "Peanut butter surprise!" he'd said, setting it down with a lot of unnecessary flourish.

Piper had stared. "What's the surprise?"

"Kent, this is literally just like an inch of peanut butter. On a saucer." There weren't even spoons.

"Exactly! It's called one-ingredient cooking. I came up with it. Kariss is gonna put it on Pinterest."

Piper had sent Jay a beseeching look like *What do we do?* Then JJ had spoken the word "Surprise," in an almost scholarly tone and thrust his entire small hand into the peanut butter because JJ Peeper was an absolute genius.

That was the high point. From there, Kent had candles and meaningful looks and used the term "double date" a lot and made eyes at Jay and Piper like a waiter at a fancy restaurant who'd been slipped a few bills to hide the engagement ring in the lady's glass. Not that subtlety had ever been Kent's strong point, but for crying out loud, there had been violins coming from the sound bar.

Kariss was zero help. She sat there and drank Sprite out of a glass bottle and smirked like it was all for her amusement.

Piper handled it surprisingly well. She ignored it with resolute splendor. She let JJ sit on her shoulder on the sofa and point to dinosaurs in the book on her lap and call them all "Dinobot." She didn't flinch when Kent suggested with all the slyness of a cartoon villain that she and Jay would be on the same team for a game of Bananagrams—which didn't even have teams. And she took the tour of Kent's extensive phone collection with what he could only call aplomb. Her responses to the candles and the violins were, in order, "Oh, would you look at that? Ambient lighting," and "So is this Tchaikovsky? Sorry, I don't know what I'm talking about. I shouldn't pretend to know things about culture."

If there were times her cheeks went pink and she looked terribly awkward at the implication that they were an item, he missed them completely. Which was a shame. And it was all Kent's fault because the times Piper might have been blushing were probably the times Jay couldn't look at her at all because he could feel the blood rushing to his face. He'd been stuttering or changing the subject or glaring at his best friend's too-innocent face. Jay was pretty sure he did not blush attractively. He was more sure that he didn't blush at all. Ever.

But here was this note. With this present. And it seemed suddenly apparent that he'd never looked at Kent or any of them and said, "Bro, we're not dating. We're just friends." Which was all true, and he'd never said it. Never said, "Kent, she's leaving soon anyway, and there's no point." Never pulled Kent aside to tell him, "You have to take it down fifty notches. I like her, but I'm really not interested." Because Kent would've backed off if he'd said that. Immediately. Except that it…wasn't entirely true, was it?

He was a little bit interested. And now that he knew that, it was becoming very difficult to remember that he could not do things like run his fingers over the back of her hand or watch the way her mouth moved when she talked or brush her newly-short hair back away from her eyes, and had he ever not been attracted to her? Because now that somehow seemed impossible. He remembered very clearly thinking she looked like a half-drowned cat! She was still in his phone contacts as Swampy! *I can never tell her that.*

Wait. I should definitely tell her that.

Jay knew he could be fine about it. He could play it very cool. All he had to do was not do anything. She was leaving. She would leave and there was no reason to make anything awkward between them before that happened. He wanted her smile and her banter and that fake glare when he teased her, and none of that would continue if he opened his mouth and said, "I would like to date you, please," or "You know, regardless of your own plans and dreams and current life situation, you should stay here and not leave."

He looked down at the picture he'd laid flat in front of his feet.

The painting wasn't anything. Two feet by three feet. Thick, heavy strokes of absent artistry forming swirling shapes and pointless angles. Its color scheme consisted heavily of blue and orange—colors which he liked, though he privately pretended they were the bane of his existence. He should hate this picture. A little. But he couldn't. Because the note and the gesture and the kindness, and was she really like this all the time? And *Get a grip, Marler,* how far gone was he already for this girl?

CHAPTER EIGHTEEN

Piper tried to recall the last time she'd felt smug. It had been a rather smug-killingly long time since she'd done anything possibly deserving of the smallest iota of smugness. So the smug feeling that had her steps loose and confident and her head bobbing only slightly to an unheard but tangibly personal-prowess-indicative beat felt pretty good. Like first-snow-cone-of-summer good.

In addition, Kariss and JJ Peeper had dropped her off a half-mango/half-coconut/half-raspberry/half-math-wasn't-JJ's-best-thing shaved ice on their way home, which was literally first-snow-cone-of-summer good.

She scooped some snow into her mouth, boldly dismissive of whether her mouth would be stained red orange for the rest of the day, and strode through the gym. The gym doors had ancient, wood-panel notices which stated plainly "No food or drink in the gym" and she'd blown past them without so much as a mental doff of her mental cap. Not that anyone observed that particular rule here. They all honored an unspoken rule about the blatant disregard of that rule. But today she simply felt wonderfully, powerfully above it and so enjoyed the sweet taste of her summer flavor amalgam and the sweeter taste of a job well done.

Fundraising would never be called her thing. Asking people for money made her intensely uncomfortable. But she had, through a random encounter at Olive's and a series of bumbling phone calls, convinced the owner to cater a portion of the Fourth of July shindig for F-R-E-E. Wasn't even part of her job, but she'd done it. It felt a little like she'd just won a fight. Which was a ridiculous way to feel not least because she'd never been in a fight much less won one. So she didn't even have a frame of reference from which she could draw such a feeling.

Even so, Piper mentally stood in the center of the ring, one gloved hand held high in victory while physically she slurped snow cone juice through the thoughtfully-provided straw. The only thing that would make it better would be the look on Jay's face when she told him— which she was on her way to collect. She back-burnered her mission when she caught sight of Mary standing by the bleachers.

"Mary!" She greeted and went in for a high five that overall felt uncoordinated but satisfying.

The shorter woman seemed a tad harried, but she always did. Piper recognized Mary's harriedness because Piper could never manage her own harriedness half as well as Mary.

"Hey, sweetie." Harried, but always gracious.

"What brings you in today?" Piper was so cool and in control.

"Oh, you know. Kids wanting to play. And it's so hot out."

"Is it?" Hm. Hard to tell with a cupful of fresh, syrupy, sculpted snow and a fully blossomed sense of accomplishment.

"Listen. I wanted to talk to you." Mary set aside the papers she'd been shuffling.

"Is it about the Fourth party? Because I got that worked out." Don't mean to brag, but…She was looking forward to bragging a little.

"No. It's, ah…a little more personal." Mary shifted in a moment of uncharacteristic uneasiness. Piper didn't know the woman very well. But she'd worked with her. Several times. And seen her around more times than that. Piper had yet to see Mary look less than sure and friendly and robed in matriarchal authority.

Furthermore Piper couldn't imagine what personal matter Mary might have with her. "Oh. Okay. Sure."

"Obviously I don't believe it," Mary said in a serious tone, eyes alternating from Piper's face to the kids playing basketball on the floor in customary Mom-surveillance. "And I've said I don't. But you know this place can be a rumor mill, and I thought you should know what's being said because… Well, I just hope nobody's said anything ugly to you or Jay."

186

It didn't take much for Piper's former swagger to flee her frame. *"What are you talking about?"*

"It's not my business. It's nobody's business but yours and his. You're adults. But some people are insinuating that…with the way you two—you and Jay—have been spending so much time together, and I guess… With the way you are when you're together, some people are wondering if your relationship has ventured into the realm of what some might call inappropriate for an employer and employee."

Piper had never had the slightest reason to resent Mary. Maybe she didn't have a good reason now, but those words—delicately chosen, and, what was that, political-sounding?—coming from this woman Piper respected reacted in her like steel on flint. "I'm…sorry?"

Mary's uneasiness shifted into obvious discomfort. "I don't think you've done anything wrong. I know you two are friends. And that you've been doing a great job since you started here. I just don't want to see what is honestly a few people making off-handed comments turn into something that might reflect badly on Jay or on this place. Or on you."

Piper didn't have any idea what to say to that.

"Maybe I shouldn't have mentioned it to you. I didn't know what to say. Are you two dating?"

She dodged a flood of a thousand defensive thoughts from Whose business is this? to Why is anyone talking about us like that? to What did we do that was so "inappropriate"? She ended up hearing herself say "No," quietly and sounding more helpless and uncertain than defensive. She found a leftover smile from somewhere, some portion of herself devoted to the care and storage of pretend facial expressions. "No. Thanks, Mary. I really appreciate you telling me."

"No problem." Mary had a pained, assessing look on her face with all the hallmarks of someone who regretted saying the things just said. "You all right, hon?"

"Yeah, of course." Yeah. Of course.

"I just thought, better to hear about it from me than get caught off-guard if someone decides to make something of it."

"Oh, yeah. Totally." Was her voice too loud? Her voice seemed extra loud.

Now Mary wore her Concern Face. It was instinct for Piper—How? Why? Since when?—to flee from that sort of face.

"Yes. Thanks, Mary. I've got to run, though. But thanks." What would a professionally unaffected person say? "Thanks. I'll keep that in mind." Keep what in mind? What am I talking about?

Fortunately Piper had her retreat firmly in progress before she could be any more professional or unaffected.

This wasn't a big deal, was it? Certainly not. *Why would this be a big deal?*

Playing Mary's words back—playing Mary's implications back—Piper was definitely feeling… something. An emotion that was unpleasant and physically uncomfortable in a shifting-stomach-contents way. Because *What on earth?* People thought she and Jay were... People thought things about them? Why? They were colleagues and friends, and was this high school?

Except it wasn't high school. If it were high school she wouldn't have to worry about some baseless rumors doing serious structural damage to her friend whose current family-based career was built on his reputation.

It was stupid. It was so stupid. She should have asked Mary more questions about who and how and why and what. But what did any of that matter? She could guarantee that whoever it was didn't know her or anything about her. Didn't know anything about who she was or where she was going or what she had lost. And Jay was a really nice guy. What, they thought she'd seduced him like he was an idiot and she was some dark mistress of the night?

Why would they think these things?

Is this my fault? It wasn't. Of course it wasn't. She hadn't done anything. Piper had been perfectly... if not professional at the very least platonic. Good grief, she was still getting over the collapse of the relationship between her fiancé and her. Why would—?

Except, what if, though? Piper had been a wreck since she arrived in Silas Bend. And she'd been lonely and grieving and lost, and Jay had been there. Kind and comfortable and helpful and friendly. And she had soaked that up. Maybe she had given people reason to talk.

Embarrassment flooded from her chest to her face. Did Jay think she was acting too flirty or whatever? Did he know what people were saying? For all she knew, he hadn't told her because he was so awfully nice and figured it would resolve itself when she left. What if he felt as awkward as she did right now?

Piper shook her head. It was difficult, but she managed not to make any frustrated noises. Silas Bend was supposed to be a short stop on her way to somewhere else. She wasn't supposed to be here long enough for anything to get bizarre or complicated. And she wasn't even supposed to be emotionally capable of being interested in someone else like some kind of emotional harlot. And she wouldn't have thought she noticeably was. Interested. Well. If she was, it was supposed to be like a crush at youth camp. Harmless and short-lived and with the understanding that there wasn't any point.

Ugh, she'd bought him wall art!

"Miss Piper!" Piper looked in the direction of the voice. A blonde-headed elementary girl pointed at Piper's snow cone. "We're not supposed to have those in here."

Piper threw the snow cone away. *I'm an idiot.*

The cursor blinked steadily in his private message box. Jay watched it, fingers settled on the keys. Of all the things he had to do today, he didn't think this would be the one that would draw on his limited time-and-effort reserves. Just a quick message. Through Facebook, even.

He wanted to write, *Hey, Jordan, really appreciated your sermon yesterday. Thanks for serving Jesus, man.* A quick aside to his pastor before he forgot. A little encouragement because Jordan Lane was a good guy and an excellent pastor, and Jay really had liked the sermon.

The problem—and it shouldn't be a problem—came in the form of his fingers itching to type something more along the lines of, *Please take me with you. For the literal love of the literal God, please take me with you.*

Yesterday Jordan spoke on Ephesians 2:10—"For we are his workmanship, created in Christ Jesus for good works, which God prepared beforehand, that we should walk in them."—and how God had a purpose for everyone, etcetera. Great and refreshing and a nice reminder, but at the end, while he was giving the announcements, he also talked about the mission trip to West Africa they'd be doing in November. Little village. No church. People who needed Jesus the way Jay needed Jesus but with no one telling them about Him.

One of the things Jay really liked about Garden Road Church was how there was always one group or another either talking about going on a trip or talking about just getting back from a trip. They went to the ends of the Earth, his church. But every now and again, wow, he wished he could just go.

Wasn't even a financial issue. He knew he could raise the support if he needed to. The time, though. Ten days off. He'd tried that once. He had not tried it since.

Days like this made it hard not to feel a little bitter—How messed up is that?—about SBCC. He shouldn't feel bitter. He had a job he was good at, that paid the bills, that he was pretty sure made his community a better place to be. But he found it difficult not to feel tied down or trussed up, found his heel bouncing or his fingers tapping, body thrumming with a feeling just shy of trapped. And he tried very hard not to ask himself *Is this even what you want?* Because it was what he had. It was what his father built. There was a legacy there. It was beautiful and good. If he couldn't be grateful for it, what kind of monster was he?

Jay pushed himself away from the computer, rolling his desk chair back until it bumped the wall. Didn't really have time for this. He glanced at Piper's painting, hanging above his green kibble couch. Wondered idly what she might say if he said the words, "What if I did something not Silas Bend Community Center?" out loud to her.

Piper had asked him once if he'd thought about it. He'd been more vague than evasive, which was still more honest than he'd let himself be on the subject lately. She'd asked about his passions, and he'd mostly shrugged because it should be this and it wasn't.

He'd never discussed it with anyone else. If he told Kent he might want something else, Kent would support him enthusiastically, but Kent's enthusiasm tended to be loud and overzealous and easily overheard. People could be touchy about things like that, and if it got around he was thinking about leaving SBCC, it would likely be a mess of hurt feelings.

Maybe Shawley and Calvin would understand.

But then they'd loved his dad so much, and maybe they'd think him as ungrateful and whiny as he felt. The whole thing would be pointless anyway because he couldn't think seriously about leaving. So there. If anything, he just needed to vent. Maybe after school started he'd take a long weekend. Get his head back in the right place.

A knock on the door frame forced his attention away from the artwork. Piper stood there in the open doorway. His face smiled at her without waiting for his consent. "Hey. You. Good, I needed to talk to you about between 60 and 85 different things."

Her face puzzled into a frown. "Is one of them term life insurance?"

"What?"

"What?"

Jay shook his head and beckoned her. "Come in."

Piper didn't move from the doorway. "Ah, I'm fine. Here. Just wanted to let you know we got Olive's Café offer to cater for us at the Fourth of July bash. I can e-mail you the details on that. Also…"

"What? That's awesome! Are you serious?"

She didn't seem nearly as happy as her news warranted. "Yes. And I was going to talk to you, too, about my replacement. Have you been doing interviews at all, or do you need me to find some applicants or…? Because I sort of doubted I'd be here this late."

Her tone as much as her words surprised him. He wouldn't have called it unkind. He would've called it…businesslike, maybe? Which wasn't like her. "Oh. Ah…"

"Not that I mind. It's been great, and I still really appreciate it. And if you need me until the end of the summer, that's still fine, but we're getting into July now. So…if you're going to hire someone, you probably want to do it soon so we can get them trained before the summer's done."

Leaving. She was talking about leaving. Well, of course, that was the plan. She didn't actually live here. She was new and temporary, and had he managed to forget that in the last half hour? "Yeah. No, you're right. You're right. I will work on that this week."

"Great. Let me know what you need from me."

"Sure. Priority number two. Priority one: I need to lock down a bounce house I should've secured a month ago for that back-to-school block party." He moved to shuffle papers on his desk. She couldn't see, could she, that they were mostly drawings gifted to him by various children?

"I already did that. Invoice is in your e-mail."

"Oh," he said. "Good."

"Yeah." She pointed over her shoulder with both thumbs. "Well, I'm going to head back downstairs."

"Cool. Uh, hey. Are you…?" He made a vague gesture. "Everything okay?"

Her eyebrows rose and her lips pressed together. "Mmhm," she said, her voice overtly perky.

"Good. Because if you need a break…"

"Of course I need a break. You need a break. Everyone who's ever been involved with this place needs a break. There honestly may not be enough Kit-Kats on the planet for the amount of breaks we need."

They looked at each other for an uncomfortably long moment. None of this was the way conversations with her usually went.

"Do you want to sit on the couch?" he offered slowly.

She looked at it a moment but didn't move from the doorway. "No."

"I don't…I don't have any Kit-Kats so…"

"Yeah, no, I'm good. Just kidding. Making the jokes. Heh. So okay, just keep me in the loop on the various loops we've got going. I'll go through any job applications we've got on file in the office and bring them up later. You won't be here then. I'll just leave them on the couch."

"Thanks."

"You're welcome." With another expression that could have been called a smile by someone without any real-world smiling experience, Piper left.

Okay. Okay, great. Everything was obviously fine. Furthermore, *What was that about?*

Piper sat cross-legged next to Hubcap on the floorboards of Shawley Bea's enormous porch, listening to the sounds of night creatures and being snacked on by flying vampiric insects. Her phone sat in front of her. She watched it while she mentally rehearsed the message she wanted to leave Laurel. Piper didn't do well leaving messages without sounding like a rambling fool when she didn't feel emotionally compromised. There was no way she was going to try to do this off the cuff. It would be better if she tried to write it out first. But then there would be evidence that she honestly couldn't do something as simple as leave a phone message for her sister without over-thinking it to death. Good grief. She'd even over-thought that.

What's up, sister? No.

Hey, girl. I just wanted to… Mm. *Hey, girl* would be overdoing it. She shouldn't try to force a tone of camaraderie. It would be unconvincing.

Hi, Laurel, it's me, Piper. Of course that's what she would say, why was she rehearsing the greeting?

Just wanted to call and check in. I don't think I'll be staying in Silas Bend much longer. Should she ask *How are things?* It seemed ludicrous to ask something like that over a phone message when the person couldn't reply to it. Asking how things were wasn't the point of the message. Laurel wouldn't be all, *Boy, I better call Piper*

196

back right away to tell her how things are! But then, it might be a manners issue, too. Phone etiquette.

Piper cursed her mercurial generation for being lax on something as vital as the rules of interfamilial phone etiquette.

If you're still okay with it, I'd still like to stay with you. I won't have a lot of rent money available, but I'll have my car done so I can job hunt ASAP. Let me know what you're thinking. Sorry about all the phone tag. [Insert painful forced laughter]

That would have to do. It was loads better than the first draft which had included tons more mental asides and a lot of *Everything I touch dies!* among other favored histrionics. Seemed that was as good as it was going to get. She picked up her phone, took a deep breath, and called Laurel.

It rang. There was a click. Then, "Hello?"

She'd answered. What? She had no mental notes for this. "Laurel!" she said, too strongly, followed by weak laughter. "Hey, I was just gonna call you."

A pause on the other end of the line. "You did call me."

"Yes. Right. Too true."

"No, it's great. I was actually going to call you. Uh, there was some shuffling. If you don't mind starting first of August, you can have a job with sales. It'll be second shift, part time. So if you still want it, you need to call. Do you still have their info?" How did Laurel sound so casual all the time?

197

"Ahhhh…yes."

"Oka—"

"How are things?" she interjected with so much etiquette as to be almost impolite.

"Fine. You?"

There are a million stories I want to tell you about Mark and Silas Bend and Hubcap and Jay and how I might be a naïve idiot and how I want to go home and where is that exactly and I'm just so tired of not knowing what in the world I'm doing, but I can't tell you any of those things because you're another one of the things I messed up. "Fine," she managed.

"Okay. Did you need anything else?"

"Nope. Just calling to let you know I still planned to stay if you're okay with it."

"Fine with me."

"Great. Everything's fine then."

"Mmhm." It was the first time they'd spoken in almost two months. Perhaps because when they talked they sounded like strangers. Except Laurel sounded like that really was all fine.

"So," Laurel said, "I guess I'll talk to you later? 'Night."

Say something else! She heard herself say, "Goodnight," and that was all.

Piper disconnected the call. She wanted to throw her phone as far as she could and hear it smash into a thousand pieces. But then she wouldn't have a phone. She wanted to bang her head against the porch railing. But then she wouldn't have an uninjured head. In the end she lobbed her phone gently into the grass in an egg-toss fashion and then went immediately to retrieve it.

CHAPTER NINETEEN

Exactly when Piper had gotten comfortable with ten-year-old boy culture, she could not say for certain. She could, however, now say for certain that Noah Porter could burp the entire roster of the Silas Bend Terrapins in alphabetical order faster than anyone else on the team.

"Braden Auger, Kolby Jasper, Kollin Jasper, Wayne Keleher, Dillon King, Amos Layhe, Chase MacKenzie, Arthur Milner, Noah Porter, Finn Tomlinson," in a steady stream of belches that would make few mothers proud and earned him the coveted prize of a second cupcake. Dillon had won for highest decibel level. Wayne for longest sustained burp. Finn seemed pleased because of something about a gag reel montage.

It wasn't as if she was competing with them.

And she had taught them the word decibel. And eructation.

I am a great coach.

She made sure to punctuate the competitions with post high-five phrases like "Don't do this at home," "Use good manners generally," and "Love is not rude." And they had done a lovely job in their scrimmage and loved her (Shawley's) chocolate cupcakes. Also, Arthur—chubby-cheeked sweetheart that he was—proudly gave her a neon green plastic whistle that he won at a Chuck E. Cheese during his family vacation, and she'd been almost embarrassingly touched.

After the past three days of feeling out of sorts and out of place, it was nice. Spending an hour being a coach. She knew where she stood with her players now, and aside from genuinely liking them most of the time, it was nice to be somewhere she knew exactly her position and purpose and had gathered something of an understanding of method. Everything about coaching her team had clear parameters. Teach basketball and get exercise and have fun and try to impart wisdom. No need to second-guess her every interaction.

If only the rest of her life could be so straight-forward. Ever since Monday's chat with Mary, Piper felt uneasy. She wished she could be the kind of person who could let that kind of thing go. Or at least do a better job of ignoring it. But now every time she was with Jay, she was thinking. Thinking and hyper-aware and sec-ond-guessing and *Are we standing too close?*

She couldn't even talk normally around him. Like she suddenly forgot how to use her vocal cords so her voice came off sounding screechy and over-forced or man-level low in an attempt to sound super casual. It was embarrassing and terrible, and all of it was so silly.

"Hey, Arthur."

The boy tipped his chin up from what was left of his cupcake to look at her. "What?"

"My voice sounds normal to you, right?"

He thought about the question with a serious expression, but ended with an ineloquent, "Uh, yeah?"

Excellent. No pressure. Just a bunch of people not worrying about what other people were thinking. It seemed excessively odd that of all things, she should find her basketball practice relaxing. Ironic that the thing she thought would lead to her requiring therapy ended up being therapeutic.

The fireworks tent was huge, a massive yellow and white affair that came and went every Independence Day season. It took a solid half-hour drive to get there, but they had the best prices Jay could find locally, and he knew the owner to throw in a few freebies for Jay's community event. Large box fans pushed humid air around, but even though it was too hot, the colors and enthusiasm kept the atmosphere light. It seemed less crowded than Jay had come to expect so close to the Fourth.

Kent bounced as Jay perused rows of aerial fireworks. "Dude, I still don't see why I can't just make the fireworks at home this time."

"We're going to have a talk about responsible Internet use later on," Jay answered as he piled a couple of packs of smaller rockets on the cake firework Kent had in his arms.

"No, seriously. Like I could really do it, though. And it would be awesome. And cheaper, probably. Way. And I have a lab coat from three Halloweens ago, and it's just been sitting in the closet, bro. Just sitting there waiting for science!"

"Yes. It sounds awesome. But A: We don't have enough time to experiment on fireworks. And B: If you blow yourself up, do you know who has to tell Kariss? Me."

Kent waved the thought away, his only rebuttal: "The police could tell her."

"It would still be my fault. And you know Kariss is like a sister to me, but deep down, at my core, I am terrified of her. I can't even be ashamed of that. I am more terrified of her than explosions."

Kent smiled a touched smile. "Aww. You should tell her that. She'd love to hear it from you."

Jay didn't know what to say. He shrug/nodded because, yes, she probably would.

"Oh. We should get some of the big, fountainy ones. For sure. Does Piper like fireworks?"

That was Kent being subtle. Jay could always recognize Kent Being Subtle because it involved 85% more eyebrows than Regular Kent—who honestly involved 85% more eyebrows than other people. "Don't know. She hasn't said." The idea of mixing Piper with fireworks seemed a terrible one. She'd managed to lose a significant portion of her hair riding a bicycle. Even if she was adamant that was an isolated incident, introducing low-grade explosives to her current impressive disaster streak seemed unwise. He liked her hair the way it looked now.

"You got a face," Kent accused, overjoyed. "You've got a thinking-about-her face."

"I do not have any idea what you're talking about. And I'm not talking to you as long as you use your fourth grade, kissed-a-girl-on-the-playground voice." Jay politely waved away an offer of assistance from a tent employee.

Kent rocked on his heels and let a beat go by before he volunteered, "Today's Word of the Day was 'besotted.'"

"No, it wasn't."

"Do you know what 'besotted' means? Because I do. Because of my Word of the Day app."

"If I tell you it's cool with me for you to mix volatile elements in your basement for the Fourth of July party, will you stop talking to me?" Jay decided to focus on the label on a pack of Roman candles.

204

"I wouldn't build the fireworks in the basement. Dude. I'd do it in the shop. On the roof maybe. Weather-permitting. And I don't get why you're being so weird about it. I mean, you like her, right? And you had the double date with us the other night."

"Not what it was."

"And I'm just saying, if you want her to be your lady fair, you have to step up your man game and tell her."

Jay straightened and turned to look at Kent. "'Lady fair?'"

"Yeah. You know who my lady fair is? Kariss. Man. She is super fair. Fairest Kariss."

"Stop."

"You're going to, aren't you? Date her? Because I know exactly two things in this situation. One: that you like Piper. And two: the definition of 'besotted.'"

"Kent. Yes," he admitted. Because he didn't know how not to, and it would be easier in the long run anyway. "Yes, I like her. But you..."

He should have more thoroughly considered the fact that they were in a public place because then Kent— unable to throw his hands in the air, loaded down as they were with stable, decorative bombs—leapt into the air. "Right! I knew it!"

"Kent."

"I did, though! That's awesome!"

"If you've ever cared about me, you will lower your voice, man."

"I know, I know," he whisper-shouted. "I'm trying." He nodded and smiled widely and still seemed to want to leap. "But dude."

"This is a thing you can't share with people."

"Why? Bro, just ask her out. You remember what I said to Kariss that faithful day?"

"Fateful. I remember what you said to Kariss. But tha—"

"And she is my wife now."

"Yes. But I'm not going to have a wife. I mean, I'm not... She's... Me and Piper won't work."

"Why? Because she's moving away? Dude." Jay had never heard a 'dude' from him sound more reproachful. "You have a phone; she has a phone. You got a car; she's got a car. That I fixed. So I know it works. Come on. Don't make a whole sad thing out of this. Just be like, 'Hey. I'm interested in you. Romantically.'"

"That is brilliant. That is a brilliant plan. However. I'm pretty sure I've already freaked her out." Jay looked around. He needed to find something else to pretend to find endlessly fascinating. He re-stacked packs of bottle rockets that were already aligned.

"What do you mean?" Kent asked.

"I guess she figured out I'm interested in her. Romantically."

"Well, yeah. Everybody knows."

"No. Everyone? Really?" Jay rolled his eyes skyward but went ahead and resigned himself to that. "Fantastic. Apparently I haven't been very subtle. That's perfect. But no. She's been… She's making it obvious she's not interested."

"What? Hold up." Kent screwed his face in such sudden, intense confusion it should've included a record scratch sound effect. "Dude, that's not possible."

"It is possible. And it's fine." Or it should have been. It felt distinctly not fine.

"She said she wasn't into you?"

"No. She's perfectly pleasant. And we're adults, and it doesn't matter. You know what my life is like. I would be terrible long-distance anyway."

"No, you wouldn't."

"It is what it is."

Kent made a scolding clicking sound with his mouth. "That is useless-human logic."

"Well," he shrugged, "it's not wrong." This was not a fireworks store conversation. Did anyone care about that?

"I don't get it," Kent said, mostly to himself, and that made Jay put the effort into quirking a smile.

"Appreciate it."

"I really thought she was into you."

Jay had been starting to think that, too. And as much as he told himself it didn't matter, wouldn't have worked, everything would continue on, etcetera, he had yet to come upon a cure from thinking about her and the way she smiled and the way she surprised him and the way he wanted to be allowed to make her laugh all the time.

"You wanna talk about it?" Kent ventured.

"No." He wanted to stop thinking about it.

"I'm just very disappointed." Kent could do sad as big as he could do happy. Puppies wept at Kent's sad face. It was made even worse for its rarity.

Jay sighed inwardly. He tried for a moment but ultimately failed not to ask, "Do you want to talk about it?"

"Yes."

CHAPTER TWENTY

Fourth of July weekend went off with scarcely a hitch. Piper spent a large portion of the event painting images on children's faces. Her most popular request was a small, happy turtle that looked a little like a green dog. The reason for its success may have had something to do with Hubcap sitting next to her in his redecorated box, looking more American than a bald eagle. He was a big hit. That turtle had winsomeness coming out his reptilian pores.

Kariss worked across from her, painting kids' faces to look like fairy tiger princesses and fire dragons and Fourth of July ninjas. Her line tended to be longer than Piper's.

Piper avoided Jay the rest of the weekend. She didn't mean to. It just seemed the better option. She couldn't be too forward or too awkward or too standoffish if he wasn't in range. It felt like a poor plan.

She missed their banter, and she missed his face. And it wasn't impossible she missed him. Not in the hurt, slightly begrudging way she missed Mark. She missed Jay…differently. Even so, it made her feel foolish.

"Piper?" Jay stuck his head into the office. Piper realized she'd been staring unseeingly at an empty clipboard on the counter. "Volunteers are here. You want to play aircraft marshal and" —he gestured with a sweeping of arms— "guide them in?"

"I'll need two flashlights and a reflective vest. And a great pair of noise-canceling headphones."

"I can get you a glow-in-the-dark football and some sticky tack."

"Done." She sent out the necessary commands for her brain to twitch her lips into a facsimile of a smile, and stood to follow Jay out. He reached out, and for one single, split second, she thought he was reaching for her hand and why would he—? But of course, he just grabbed a pen out of the holder on the desk and stuck it behind his ear. Because of course. Piper did follow him out of the office then, and added paranoid and delusional to her mental list of All the Different Types of Idiot Piper Can Manage to Be in One Day.

She didn't want him to hold her hand anyway.

It wouldn't be appropriate.

And he wouldn't. That was the point. She really needed to remove herself from the whole situation. Post haste.

For the month of July, Silas Bend Community Center acted as one of several drop sites around town for a back-to-school book drive. A large cardboard box with a printed sign had been sitting at the front entrance to collect used books. Once the books were sorted roughly by type and reading level, school teachers in the area would have first crack at them for their classroom libraries. Then from 6:00-8:00 that evening, the doors would open to the rest of the public, and the books would sell for a quarter a pop. The local library had shut down three years ago. The book drive had been an annual thing at SBCC since.

As Piper organized the half-dozen volunteers to set out rows of long tables in the gym and sort through boxes of books, she considered everything she had here. She liked it. Even with every circumstance that left her wrong-footed three miles from her comfort zone, she realized that this was the first time she'd really gotten to use what God had given her—her practical side and her glaringly impractical side to do things she felt were worth doing. To serve people. To serve the Lord in serving people. She got to do things that left her exhausted but fulfilled. Even when she was with Mark, when she was working toward molding her life into what she thought it should be, she never felt as excited about what she was doing.

Had she ever felt like she was good at something?

Piper had always heard about seeking God's will and following God's will and knowing God's will. From the time she'd become a Christian, she thought she had that pretty well down. But now, suddenly it seemed apparent that she wasn't even sure what it meant.

A few months ago, she would've been plenty confident that her relationship and her job and her set course were a hundred percent a product of following God's will. Because she'd planned it out. But that was all gone now, and it was painfully apparent that she'd been smack dab in the middle of her own plan, not God's. Scarier, she knew that had she been left to her own devices, she'd still be there. It hadn't been God's voice she'd heard that got her out of there. It had been Mark's.

"Are you having a breakthrough?"

Piper jumped. Kariss stood next to her. "What? No. Why?"

"Your expression looks like that time at the flea market." JJ stood on the other side of Kariss. His arms were crossed, face set in an impressive scowl. Like a little tiny bouncer.

"JJ? What's that face you're making?" Piper asked.

JJ looked up at her seriously. "We hafta make sure nobody is bothering you while you breakthrough."

"Oh. Thanks." Piper explained to Kariss, "I'm not actually having a breakthrough."

"What are you having?"

"A…um…" Crisis? It wasn't really a crisis. That would be dramatic phraseology. "Thoughts. Just thoughts."

Kariss stared at her with that penetrating just-this-side-of-a-glare. JJ followed suit, which made the scene even more unsettling. He was four years old. What did he think he was looking for? To be fair, what did Kariss think she was looking for?

"Piper. Hey, Kariss. JJ."

For the first time in a week, Piper could admit she was glad for Jay's interruption, glad to see him without any mixed feelings on the subject. JJ immediately latched onto an arm and clambered up onto Jay's back with minimal aid in a move the two could execute seamlessly. "Hey, buddy."

JJ popped his lips twice and shifted dangerously to crawl up to Jay's shoulders.

A new voice lent itself to the mix. "Wow. He's quite the climber." A young blonde, perhaps a little older than Piper, though it may have just seemed that way because she was taller. She had a pleasant voice and a pleasanter face, and both were vaguely familiar.

Piper searched her memory banks and pointed uncertainly. "Emily?" she tried, squinting one eye closed.

The woman looked surprised and delighted. "Yes! I didn't know if you'd remember."

They'd only met briefly. "You were at the bike-riding thing." Piper had been preoccupied at the time.

"Yes! Your hair looks amazing."

Piper touched her hair. It wasn't difficult to sound self-deprecating. "Hair science has come a long way."

"Emily and I were talking today," Jay cut in smoothly. He seemed rather proud of himself. "Interviewing. She wants the job. She's not going to be able to make all the hours you do, but...you're kind of insane, so..."

He flashed a brief smile that should not have made her feel as pleased as it did. She'd been called insane by any number of people for any number of reasons.

"Anyway I thought, if you wanted to kind of show her what you do a few days this week, that would be awesome, and we can figure out if this is going to work for everybody long term before we start training her for real."

"Yes, of course we can." Piper turned to Emily. "It's a really fun job, most days. Busy like you wouldn't believe, but if you like that, you'll love it here."

"No, that sounds perfect." Emily seemed terribly nice. She seemed terribly nice the entire time Piper introduced her to Kariss, and the three of them plus JJ went on an abbreviated tour of the building that more served as a chance for them to get acquainted.

Emily was kind and had a direct sense of humor. A generous laugher, but in a good way. Piper liked her. She was easy to like. If her work ethic matched her congeniality, she'd be a smash.

After the books were sorted, and schoolteachers flocked to inspect the tables, Piper found herself standing by the wall near the doorway, wishing they had some sort of food spread. Not that she felt particularly hungry, but it would be something to actively manage without having to worry about long conversations with people. She didn't much feel like interacting with humans.

Emily would be her replacement. Her answer to prayer. It shouldn't have felt odd, but it did. Piper had even said some plain version of "We need to get my replacement in here so I can peace out, thanks." But then…Emily. Who was a real person, who would be doing Piper's job. Not Piper's job. The job Piper had been borrowing from the start. The job she'd been allowed to babysit. A seat she'd kept warm.

Jay had been doing her a favor letting her work, and there was no reason to feel anything but gratitude as she prepared to leave. How could one person be so incomprehensibly bad at change? It wasn't even as if the change had crept up on her. She knew she'd be leaving. She wanted to leave. So why was she suddenly looking with morose fondness on the scuffed gym floor and the dingy paint on the walls?

Jay and Kariss and Kent and JJ and Shawley and Calvin and everyone else she'd met would go on with their lives. It wasn't like Piper wanted them to remember her. It was like Piper hated fiercely that she would miss out on them.

Across the room, Jay looked up and made eye contact, startling her, possibly him as well. He scooped a stack of books into his hands before striding over to meet her. His steps slowed as he approached. Was it part wariness? She hated the thought that the way she'd acted the last week might have made him wary of her.

I am messing everything up. If she left Silas Bend with the one person she was most grateful to, the one person—if she was perfectly honest—she would miss the most, thinking she was anything but grateful, she should not be allowed to be around people. If anyone deserved her thanks and her…her fondness, Jay Marler did.

Jay stood next to her, tilting his body toward the room. "Hey." He gave her an innocuous smile.

"Hey."

"This thing gets bigger every year somehow."

Oh gosh, it was small talk. They'd been reduced to small talk.

"Really? That's surprising." She wasn't even sure it was. She watched him rock back on his heels. "I'm not upset with you, you know," she blurted.

His bland expression stretched into surprise. "Oh. Good." He seemed to think on that a moment. "Was that…? Were you considering being upset with me?"

"Nope."

"Great," he nodded.

She really needed to learn the ancient art of tact.

"You know," he said, "Kent's been on this 'word of the day' kick."

"Oh?"

"Yep. So…if you needed a good definition of 'non-sequitur'…"

"Right." She might've grinned. But it also might have been a grimace. "Sorry. No. Ha. That was one, wasn't it? Sorry about that. No, I wanted to thank you, actually."

Jay stared at her. "This conversation is an emotion tornado."

"Sorry. But really. I was… When we first met, I didn't exactly have my best foot forward. All my best feet were covered in mud and rain and…crazy."

He didn't seem to be completely following her, but he didn't disagree either. "How many best feet do you have?"

"I'm sure I didn't come across as particularly trustworthy or…stable. But you gave me this opportunity, and you went out of your way to make sure I had what I need. And not just that, but this. This job. It's been good, you know? Like I would've been lucky to end up washing dishes somewhere to earn enough to fix my car and camping in a ditch to save all my dishwashing pennies."

"Well camping would never have worked. I don't think Hubcap cares much for nature."

"But you gave me responsibilities," she went on. She had to ignore him if she wanted to have any chance of getting any of this to come out right. "You set me up doing ministry really. Which I didn't even realize how much I would love. I get to be passionate about what I'm doing, even when I'm out of my element. I've been challenged, and I've learned a lot. It's been wonderful.

217

It's not something I would have chosen, and it's just been so...like nothing I've ever done before. The whole thing, a godsend. I mean a literal," she mimed taking something from Heaven and placing it on Earth, "Godsend. So thank you."

"I'm glad." He did look a bit verbally windswept.

"Right." Piper winced. "Emotion tornado."

"No, it's fine. Tornados have their place. Ask Dorothy Gale. From Kansas. Hers worked out for her."

"Mm." Stretching a little. But graciously.

"So, you like Emily?"

"I like Emily." She tried not to sound miserable as she said it. She didn't know whether liking Emily made it better or worse.

"Good. I thought you would." He scratched a blunt fingernail across the pages of one of the books in his hands.

"What are you doing with those books?"

Jay looked down at them with a bewildered expression. "I. Don't. Know," he said. "I just picked them up. To look busy I think? I'm going to go..."

"Yes. Keep going. Put them down somewhere."

"Yes." He pressed his lips together briefly, and his face pulled itself into several painful-looking directions. But then he met her eyes. "You're a godsend, too. So. Yeah. You are, too."

218

She fought against an unreasonable warmth she felt flood her face. "And Hubcap," she pointed out to deflect.

"Definitely a godsend." He looked like he might have said something else, but he cut himself off with a sweet, close-mouthed smile. Gave her a little wave and took off.

She stood there a moment, mentally preparing a crop of convincing happy thoughts before she could reintroduce herself into the company of people. Kent popped up before she had a chance to move.

He stopped on his way to wherever he was going and wheeled around to face her. "Oh, hey, Pi."

"Hi, Kent."

He examined her closely within a handful of seconds. Shockingly, instead of a thousand words, he settled on a very succinct, "You look sad."

"Kariss said I looked thoughtful," she half-complained.

"Wistful," he decided. "Definitely wistful." He considered for a moment. "You want a hug?"

Piper nodded and tried not to do it heavily. Next thing, she was in the center of a hug that felt miraculously sincere. While it should have amused her, she felt the absurd urge to cry. Stifled it. "Thank you," she huffed.

"Pass it on, right?" he nodded with conviction, and that caught her off guard enough to overtake the cry-reflex.

She closed her eyes briefly. "Right."

"Everything…good?" he checked as she pulled back.

"Oh, you know. Yeah."

"We're going to head out and get doughnuts," he said. "You want to come?"

"No, I think I'll stick around here for the duration. Thanks, though."

"All right. I'm gonna go track down my wife and the product of our love."

Piper raised an eyebrow. "You don't call him that in front of him, do you?"

CHAPTER TWENTY-ONE

As long as Jay could remember, Calvin Hayes' breakfast order had been two eggs poached, sausage links not patties, fresh fruit, and two apple pancakes. Jay had no idea how eggs were poached or why anyone would call it that.

But it didn't stop him from ordering for his older friend. Jay had anomalously arrived at the diner early. It didn't suit his mood—this being early business. He didn't see what anyone saw in it. Jay did his best not to be late to his engagements, but sitting and waiting for something to start had never been his forte.

Calvin arrived eventually—on time—and the two went through the pleasantries that were necessary because it had been awhile since they'd had breakfast together. After the food arrived, Calvin prayed, and it calmed Jay, listening to the man's familiar, steady voice and the reminder of why Jay wanted to talk to him.

"I love Silas Bend Community Center. I love everything my dad built it to be," he said carefully. "What would you think if I didn't run it anymore?"

He watched Calvin's face. For a look of betrayal or disappointment or hurt. Because Jay felt a little like a betrayer for saying it. Could imagine a look like that on his dad's face, and it made him feel sick. If anyone had reason to feel let down or wounded by Jay's talk of giving SBCC up, it would be Calvin. He'd known Jay's dad back when the community center was a dream. He'd been part of the struggle to make it real. Calvin and Jay's dad had been like Jay and Kent, with the caveat that no one could be like Kent. After Jay's dad died, Calvin was there, always.

Calvin sat on his side of the booth, quietly regarding Jay. But there was no sign of disgust or disappointment. He said, "Tell me more."

"I'm not talking about shutting it down. Not if I can help it. I'm talking about going somewhere else. Doing something else."

"You know you work too many hours there. If you're burned out, you're burned out. Frankly it's amazing it's taken you this long. But if you're talking about making a life-altering decision, I think you need to take a step back first. Really think about what all that would mean. I don't know a man who ever made a big decision in his exhaustion he didn't regret afterwards."

"I might be exhausted," Jay admitted. He'd been doing exhaustion as a lifestyle. That was probably a mistake, too.

"What is it you're wanting to pursue?"

"I don't even know. Completely."

"You want me to tell you it'll be okay." Calvin shook his head, not unkindly. "I don't know. I really don't, Jay. I don't know that encouraging you to do what you're talking about is the right thing or not. I'm sorry. I know that's not what you want to hear. But whatever you do, I know God is in control. He'll open the doors or close them. Your job is to be obedient. To go where He leads you. To stay where He places you. Do you think God is calling you to go somewhere else?"

That question people were always throwing around in church. "I could stay. I really think I could. I could stay and run SBCC forever. Until I retire. Or until I just can't anymore. I could do that and be fine. But that's the thing. Am I being called to live a life that's fine? I'm not trying to romanticize anything. I get plenty of adventure where I am. It's just...Piper said something to me. About how working at the community center challenged her and about how it fit with where her passions are."

"Piper, hm?" Calvin asked, equal parts musing and knowing.

"Or we could not talk about that right now." Jay cut off Calvin's tone at the knees. Bad enough Kent was moping around about how things were with Piper. "With me, the center seems like the opposite of where my passions are. I mean, it's still... It'll always be challenging. But I'm looking around, taking stock, and this is not what I'm passionate about. It's just...everything I've always done. I know God does not call people to exactly what they would like to be doing all the time. I mean… Jonah, right? And I'm not saying I want to jump on a boat to Tarshish if this really is what He has for me. I just…I am suddenly unconvinced that it is. Like I want to go to Ninevah. I just have no idea where it is." Jay took a deep breath. "Tell me if I'm being young and stupid."

"What would you say if I told you you were?"

"I don't think I am." Jay held his hands up and then dropped them in his lap. "But do you think I am?"

"No. I don't think you are. Seeking what God wants for your life is the opposite of young and stupid. I just, hmm…" Calvin set his fork down gently. "I think I hate change. Suddenly." He sounded reluctantly amused. "I'm not sure how that happened. Not sure when it happened. So, I'll be honest, my knee-jerk response to what you've just said is to shoot down anything that isn't you living here in town, nearby, eating Sunday dinner with me and Shawley, and getting your name in the paper all the time for this or that thing SBCC's doing." Calvin shook his head and searched Jay's face. "Don't let me do that, Jay."

"I'll try."

"Wherever you go," he said, "I'm cheering you on."

Jay nodded. "I know."

224

The high school band planned to host a 5k run fundraiser Saturday morning, early. It was the sort of thing Jay didn't have to have his hands on. The band director and his students handled the planning, food, and announcements. But he did have to clear a spot in the office for the boxes of event t-shirts.

Piper and Emily were already in the office, sitting in swivel chairs and refolding a box of t-shirts that had apparently gotten smashed and scattered outside in a mishap that heavily featured Piper, the hand truck, and a near-miss with an as yet unnamed person's Lexus. The two women appeared to be getting along swimmingly. He found himself feeling optimistic that Emily would work out. Longer than three months would be ideal.

Optimism about the new employee took some of the focus off the heaviness crowding in from the ever-expanding portion of his brain that wanted to think about Piper. All the time. In bizarre ways like irrational irritation because *Why wasn't I there for the hand truck thing? Hand truck adventures are ours!* and only partially joking to himself about twisting another ankle.

Jay set his box on top of the stack as his phone buzzed in his back pocket. Text from Kariss. He thumbed it open, and found a picture of JJ perched in a nest he'd made at the top of his bookshelf, wearing a dinosaur mask and sunglasses and holding a marker board that read "Sign us up for the 1 mi. walk on Sat." Kariss made texting an art. Often featuring her son. And like much of what is considered art, Jay could appreciate it without understanding it at all.

He texted her back a quick thumbs up and went to head out to grab another box when the phone buzzed again.

This time dino JJ—JJsaur? JJsaur, definitely—was hanging upside down from his bed. The marker board read, "What about you?"

Jay typed out, "Running the 5k."

He'd already been out to the truck to retrieve another box and deposit it in the office before he got another text. This time it was in an artistic black and white. A young dinosaur boy sitting pensively on a rock, staring with remarkably human eyes off into the middle distance. Alone with his thoughts. Which in this case were plainly spelled out on a white board. "What about Piper?"

That woman could text Piper herself to find out whether or not she was doing the 5k. If it had been Kent, Jay would have just texted back, *Shut up, man.* But it wasn't Kent. It was Kariss. One did not say "shut up" to Kariss Peeper. The same way one did not plug the toaster in too near the bathtub.

Since his conversation with Calvin that morning, Jay wasn't sure how he felt. Tired? He'd been early to a breakfast that was itself entirely too early. Had talking to Calvin made him feel better or worse? He appreciated Calvin. Could always trust Calvin to be honest with him. But the conversation hadn't been exactly the conversation he'd wanted, not that he knew what he'd wanted from Calvin. It left him feeling silly and unmoored. As if everything he did lately was a bad idea. As if everyone else was on the same page, and he only just then realized he'd spent the last hour making paper airplanes.

Jay stood in the office doorway doing nothing until the sound of evil, echoing laughter sprang out of nowhere and made him jump. Emily gasped from the desk.

Piper called out, "Oh, that's me," and retrieved her phone from her shorts pocket. "I got a text."

Once his heart rate slowed, he asked, "Was that Vincent Price horror-laughing?"

"It's a text from Kariss," she explained.

"Oh."

Emily shot him a look of confusion. He waved her concern away.

Jay shouldn't stand there and watch Piper read her text message. He shouldn't be loitering in the office. He did both things and saw Piper's face morph into a puzzled frown. "What?" he asked.

"It's a picture," she answered slowly.

"Of what?"

"It's a...JJsaur. Running triumphantly. In sepia tone." She tilted her head as she studied the screen. "I do not know what this means. Would a better friend know what this means?"

"Nah," he assured her.

"It is adorable." She held up an idea-inspired index finger, "I'll text her back that it's adorable."

In two weeks, she'd be gone. It was a fact, but it hardly felt real to him. Not because he couldn't picture his life without her. He could easily picture his life without her. The vast majority of his life he'd lived without her, and he'd been...fine. The thought of her leaving shouldn't hollow out his insides the way it did.

But as he studied her, sitting a few feet away, t-shirt and shorts and deceptively unremarkable, frowning at her phone, he fought the compulsion to walk over and hug her. He wanted to tell her all the things he was thinking about his life and about the Lord and about *Where do I go from here?* He didn't know what she would say, but he thought he liked hearing her voice, and *God, I didn't even realize You made people like her.*

Beautiful, with her short hair, even under fluorescent lights. And everything about her was a story.

Jay rubbed his hand through his hair. In two weeks, she'd be gone. She seemed willing to stay as far away from him as circumstances allowed—seemed to prefer it. If he had any sense at all, he'd let her. He'd spend the next two weeks systematically letting go of all the feelings he had for her.

Regardless of what Calvin said, Jay felt young and foolish.

"So I'm running in the thing," he found himself announcing. "Piper, are you running in the thing with me?"

"Sure," she answered absently as she typed. Then she looked up sharply from her phone. "Wait."

"You just agreed to run a 5k," Jay told her.

She looked utterly betrayed. "Curse upon curses. Why would I do that?"

"For the t-shirt?" he offered.

Piper looked at the box of t-shirts, considering, and then let out a happy hum. It all felt pretend. Her face was red around her smile. The tension that had left their last several interactions feeling choked was real. But he'd almost gotten used to that, and the pretending was necessary if he wanted to be near her the next two weeks. Which he resolutely, regrettably did.

"Emily?" Jay asked. Because he had not forgotten about her. "Were you planning to run?"

Emily let out a bark of laughter. "I would rather eat this box of t-shirts."

"You are a much more self-possessed woman than I am," Piper told her. "I'd like to be self-possessed like you."

Jay texted *Kariss back, She's running it, too. JJ is adorable.*

Emily was a marvelous talker. Piper loved that most about her. As Piper showed her how everything worked—or didn't work as was sometimes the case—at

SBCC, she could trust that if she trailed off thoughtfully, Emily would be there with pleasant friendly chatter about her husband, David, or his work or their house or their trip last summer or some story from college or about her favorite high school teacher who'd recently died. The last one wasn't as pleasant. But it was sincere and still helpful because it didn't leave Piper alone with her own thoughts.

Piper's thoughts were relentless.

At their most relentless, they wanted to resent Emily for her compact, sweet, understandable, anecdotal life. Which seemed an insane thing. Emily wasn't bragging. She was engaging. And if Piper had been a better person, she would've engaged back a bit more.

But Piper's stories were full of broken home and arrogant mistakes and life structural collapse. She did talk about Hubcap as if he were her child. She talked about Shawley and Calvin and how great they were. But she didn't trust her doom and gloom mood. So she mostly acted as a wall for Emily to volley words off of like a conversation racquetball. Piper would always bounce the ball right back but didn't provide the dynamic experience of another active player.

Emily volunteered to supervise teardown after evening volleyball, so Piper found herself with a rare opportunity to leave at six o'clock. Like a normal workday. In the spirit of contrariness, she didn't know what to do with her unexpected extra hours of freedom. She didn't want to go back to Shawley Bea's. They would make pleasant faces at her. She loved them. She loved their faces. But Piper feared that after several hours her smile had grown brittle, and if she tried to make her face pleasant back at them her face would crack like a china doll's. She worried they knew her well enough now to be able to tell.

She texted Kariss. Kariss wouldn't make any faces at her. Or if she did, Kariss wouldn't be bothered by not being smiled at in return. Piper sat in the driver's seat of her restored Honda and pulled the handle to lean the seat back as far as it would go before typing out a text.

Me:

>>At what level of friendship are we currently?

Piper pulled one knee up and rested it on the steering wheel. The fabric on her car ceiling was starting to droop. Is that the sort of thing you're supposed to fix? Or do you just sort of…accept it until it's time to get a new car?

Deep in her spirit, she wanted to turn that thought into some sort of analogy about life, but she fought against it. The last thing her life needed was more analogies.

Vincent Price's bone-chilling laugh startled her.

Kariss:

<<I wouldn't die for you. But I would go on vacation with you. So about an 8:10.

Huh. Piper found that touching to an absurd degree.

Me:

>>Are you free for friendship time?

She hardly had to wait for the reply.

Kariss:

<<I have JJ. Come over.

As soon as Piper arrived, she was ushered to the couch. She sat.

"Not like that," Kariss shook her head. "It should be more...devastated and fainty."

"Why?"

"You're here because you're being a romantic heroine about Jay, right? Back of the hand to the forehead and swoon. Go."

Piper ought to argue. She ought to be indignant. "I'm not doing heaving sobs."

Kariss crossed her arms. "We'll see."

Piper spent the next few moments practicing suitably dramatic sprawls across the lounge portion of Kariss's sectional. Then JJ wanted to try. In seconds, JJ had effortlessly changed the rules, such as they were, to include the floor being filled with sharks. After that, suddenly they had no time for gasping and fainting in proper Victorian theatrics because pillow warfare. JJ Peeper was a severe general. But wise.

It took Kariss some time after that to settle things down and figure out whether or not that lamp had any chance of ever becoming unbroken again.

"Sorry about the lamp," Piper said eventually, when she and Kariss were sitting on the sofa like the piece of furniture it was, chips and salsa in hand, and JJ sat busily marking up construction paper at the kitchen table.

Kariss shrugged away any responsibility Piper felt without seeming to actually move any muscles.

"So I have the look of a romantic heroine?" Piper asked.

"No. You don't. Would you like to? I have fabrics."

"Jay asked me to run in a 5k race, and I said sure."

If Piper wasn't mistaken, those were faint traces of amusement in Kariss's green eyes. "Then you need to marry that guy."

Piper let her head fall backwards onto the couch back. "That's not what I meant at all."

"You agreed to do a 5k with him. You. Clearly you have no interest in him whatsoever."

"You haven't known me long enough to make those kinds of astute observations."

Kariss's look became a degree more pointed. "I could've made that astute observation within three to five minutes of having met you."

Piper raised a salsa-covered chip to acknowledge, "That's fair."

"So what's the problem?"

"I don't have a problem," she lied blatantly.

"You are a damsel, and your corset is too tight. I can see it in your face."

"Right. Okay." Piper set her plate on the coffee table. "I shouldn't care about him. The way that I do. He's my boss. I'm still reeling from my last relationship. I'm leaving. And apparently I can't be around him without making people think he's got no integrity."

"How many of these problems go away if you consider the possibility that maybe he cares about you, too?"

"He..." Piper stopped.

"You've considered it."

"Of course." She hadn't seriously. Maybe she had, theoretically. But that would've involved thinking heavily about his feelings and his thoughts and what he might want, and she'd been much too busy trying to figure out her own mind. It was easier, anyway, not thinking about whether or not Jay might want her. "I don't trust me to make any decisions about a relationship right now."

"Okay. Who do you trust to make a decision about a relationship right now?"

"Jesus," she said stubbornly. Because she'd been to Sunday school. "It doesn't matter. I'm not going to do anything about it. And he can't do anything about it because...he's my boss. Then I'm going to move away, and I highly doubt he's going to want to be in a long distance relationship on top of the 3.8 billion things he's got going on. Everything's fine. I just feel sad. I came here because I feel sad. I know I won't feel sad forever. But right now I feel sad."

Kariss patted her shoulder and didn't say anything. Then Kariss shoved her shoulder so Piper wound up sprawled dramatically sideways again, and she found that at least she could still laugh.

The gym was buzzing with scattered groups of runners in varying stages of sleepiness. Some bounced and stretched, while most leaned against things or sipped coffee or nibbled at a banana or doughnut from one of the food tables.

A glance at his watch told Jay sunrise was still firmly in progress when Kelli Raines, a high school band member he'd known since she had started elementary school, called for all the runners' attention so she could welcome everyone and explain the route and the timekeeping and prizes, etc. People shuffled vaguely closer to listen.

Piper stood at Jay's elbow with her face in a ceramic mug of coffee.

"Did you bring that mug from home?" he asked quietly out the side of his mouth.

"Yes," she mumbled. "It's my favorite."

"Why did you bring it with you?"

"I don't think I meant to. Why are you asking me questions like I'm someone who's awake?"

"If you don't pay attention, you're going to miss all the rules," he nodded toward Kelli.

"There are rules? Do people cheat at fundraces… fundraiser races?"

"Tons of rules," he said somberly. "These things are cutthroat. You have to watch the blind turns. That's when people start throwing elbows. Especially the over-sixty age bracket. Those folks have nothing to lose, and they may resent you for your youth and beauty." He'd meant to say youth and vigor.

Piper didn't seem to notice. She weighed her heavy mug in her hand. "Well"—her voice had turned low and threatening, never mind the fact she seemed barely coherent—"I hope they've been taking their calcium supplements. They're gonna need 'em."

Jay had to bite both lips and squeeze his eyes shut to keep from laughing. Several weeks ago, this woman had been strapped into a bunch of mismatched sports gear and prepared to wreak vengeance upon the household of every turtle in the area. How had he not proposed right then?

"Dude," came a stage whisper startlingly close to his ear. Jay turned to find an excited Kent standing there as hyperactive at ten to six in the morning as he was at ten to six in the evening. JJ, in rare form, was snuggled into his dad's shoulder, all the intrepid daredevil in him hibernating in preparation for a more reasonable time of day.

"Hey," Jay greeted. "That kid knows what's up."

Kent grinned proudly and kissed the little guy's head. "He was real excited about going a mile. Even though I'm pretty sure he goes like at least fifty miles a day. He's just a sleepy little bear, though, right now."

JJ grumbled, presumably in supercilious outrage at the mere suggestion he could be a sleepy little bear, but it was muffled against Kent's collar bone.

Kariss appeared next to her husband, sipping coffee from a paper cup.

"You look the same as you always look," Piper accused. "Both of you do. Are you vampires?"

"No. We slay vampires," Kariss answered immediately.

"We would. If we had to," Kent agreed. Then he whispered "There's no such thing as vampires," into his mostly-asleep child's hair. They were the best parents Jay had ever seen.

Piper and Jay said goodbye to the three Peepers outside at the starting line. The air was comfortably warm, but a far cry from the heat they'd be facing as soon as that sun rose higher. It would be the perfect time for a run if not for the actual time.

"So, are we staying together or are we here to race?" Piper asked as she halfheartedly stood on one leg and then the other to stretch her quads.

"Staying together. Unless you decide to leave me in your dust."

"Don't patronize me."

"Got it. No, I'm staying with you. I fear the elderly elbows. And you, for some reason, are still carrying that mug."

She looked at the heavy mug still in her hands as someone ahead blew the whistle to signal the start of the race. "Blast."

Jay convinced her to leave the mug next to a newspaper stand around the one-mile mark. Around the two-mile mark, she was huffing and puffing.

"How long is a 5k? Like 26 miles?"

"That's a marathon," he told her.

"We're running a marathon? The man who ran the first marathon famously died! From running the first marathon!"

"You're not listening to me at all. But that is an excellent historical nugget, thank you." In a way, he was grateful they couldn't talk much. Because if she kept being that exasperated it was going to be very difficult to not think about kissing her, and that would do him no good.

The last quarter mile rose into a slight incline.

Piper made a sound like she'd gotten punched in the stomach. "I'm going to die here. Tell the marching band I hope it was worth it."

"It'd probably just be another feather in their cap."

"Not jokes!" she wheezed. "Don't do jokes. I need you to be inspirational. Like lay some Scripture on me or something."

"Oh. Um. I could start saying all the Bible verses they put on sports posters. 'Let us run with perseverance, the race marked out for us,' and all those."

"Yes! Brilliant! That. Truth doping. Go."

"Uhh… 'I have fought the good fight, I have finished the race, I have kept the faith.' Then there's, 'Be strong and courageous. Do not be afraid or terrified because of them, for the LORD your God goes with you.'"

"Aw yes He does!" she agreed heartily, pumping a fist in the air. "I got one."

"Do it."

"Psalm 127:2!"

"Yeah? What's that?"

"'It is in vain that you rise up early and go late to rest; eating the bread of anxious toil; for He gives to his beloved sleep!' Emphasis mine." Her grin was all cheek and chutzpah.

"I have never seen that one on a poster."

"That is the reason why we had to be here so insanely early."

"'My only aim is to finish the race and complete the task the Lord Jesus has given me—the task of testifying to the good news of God's grace.'"

"I've noticed that," she said. "You do that all the time. Even when you're not even trying. God could drop you in the vacuum of space and end up using you to start a church for astronauts."

Her words caught him straight in the chest, so unexpectedly that if he hadn't already been breathing hard from jogging and talking, he might've made an embarrassing noise. Piper just kept jogging, slowly, and talking and smirking and panting and complaining in that way she did that wasn't really complaining. She simply kept on because she couldn't have meant for her words to mean what they did to him.

My only aim is to *finish the race and complete the task the Lord Jesus has given me—the task of testifying to the good news of God's grace.* Acts 20:24

My only aim...testifying to the good news of God's grace. He'd only quoted the verse because it had the word "race" in it. Because she'd asked him to be inspiring for the final leg of the run neither of them were taking seriously. But then she flipped everything over with a simple, sweet reminder that God could use him anywhere and an unthinkingly faith-filled affirmation that He would. Such a basic truth, and Jay had been worrying and fretting and praying, and he'd overlooked that God was bigger than Jay's plans. That God wouldn't be stymied or disappointed or surprised by the decision Jay made over what to do about SBCC.

God, I want to go wherever You want me, he prayed, the same way he'd been praying. Then he added, *And Lord, wherever I go, I trust that You're already there paving the way.*

Jay hadn't expected to finish the race feeling stronger than when he started it. He glanced over at Piper, with her hair pinned back from her sweaty forehead, gamely soldiering on for no real reason. Helpless, he found himself floundering in a rush of affection for this woman who would shake her fist at the sun until it rose but would quote Bible verses back and forth with him because the Bible was what moved her.

He realized belatedly they'd stumbled their way across the finished line. The runners had spread out quite a bit during the run, but there were several who'd finished ahead of Jay and Piper gathered near the finish, talking among themselves and cheering for the racers as they came in.

"Did you hear the guy?" Piper asked, walking next to him with her hands on her head as her breathing slowed. "Our time was 33:41. Which seems impossible to me because I'm pretty sure we were running at least twenty miles per hour…"

"I want to date you." The words came without hesitation. Almost without thought except that he had thought them. Her mouth went o-shaped as her eyebrows shot up, and in the moment, even that wasn't enough to make Jay stop. "I mean, I want to take you on a romantic date. Romantically. Before you leave. Today, maybe. Tonight. I would date you tonight if I could."

Piper didn't even move to take her hands off her head. She stood there, staring up at him, sweaty and surrounded by people, and only then did it occur to Jay he may have done a bad thing. "What?" she asked eventually.

Instead of backing up in an orderly, cohesive fashion, his mouth blurted, "If not, that's fine. If you aren't there, romantically, you can say no. I won't make it weird. But, just to be as clear as I can, I am currently asking you if you would like to go on a…"

"If you use the word romantic again, I will actually, physically die." She hadn't looked away from him, but her hands finally slid from her head. She swallowed rapidly and seemed like she may not be getting enough air. She didn't look like a person who wanted to go on a date with the person who had just asked her.

Jay wished he had an idea what his face was doing. But he only knew the sharp, bitter jab of disappointment. "Oh." He already knew she didn't want to. He shouldn't have asked.

"No, I… Yes. No. Yes." She made several frantic hand motions he didn't understand. "Jay, what are you talking about? You can't date me. You're my boss."

"So what? I'm my boss, too. I mean…this isn't something I normally do. But even if you weren't leaving—which you are—I'm pretty sure I never put something in the handbook that says we can't date."

"Handbook?" She gave him an absolutely Piper look about that. As if he'd ever write a handbook. Then she shook her head. "People are going to talk."

"People are always going to talk. That's what people do. Anybody who's in a position of authority gets talked about. My parents went through it all the time. That's not going to bother me." Well, it would always bother him. But it certainly wasn't going to stop him.

"I'm moving away. You don't even know where I'll be living."

"Is it closer than, I don't know…the sun? Because even then, pretty sure we could work around it." And in that moment, he was not sure whether or not he'd just made a terribly ill-timed, inadvertent pun. If her squinty-eyed, pained expression was any indication, she was similarly unsure.

Jay took a mental step back. "I'm not… You don't have to commit to a relationship right now. Obviously. Obviously. But I'd like to take you out. If you like." He shifted and tried not to grimace. "I promise I won't say romantically again. I don't know where that came from."

She looked at him a long time. He didn't know what she was thinking. He often didn't. Her eyes watched him softly, and he tried not to fidget or look like he was trying to hurry her along, but he really didn't know what she was thinking, and unlike often, this time it was agonizing.

"Question," she finally said.

"Yes."

"Just to be clear: the sun would be too far?" she asked. "The sun is the definitive cutoff as far as long-distance relationships go?"

"Yes. Because I imagine the radiation would interfere with wi-fi coverage. And also because you'd be incinerated."

She nodded sagely like she thought him shrewd, and he never wanted her nonsense to be anywhere else. "When would you like to romantically date me?"

CHAPTER TWENTY-TWO

Piper remembered a basketball game later that morning. She remembered the Silas Bend Terrapins playing basketball. She remembered Noah Porter continuing to sulk that they should be called the Silas Bend Terror-pins, and she remembered once again explaining about branding and how that name wouldn't be as relatable to the public.

It was shameful she couldn't remember many more specifics because she thought they might even have won the game.

Her thoughts had been hijacked by Jay's face and his eyes and his blinking and his wincing and his I want to date you. Some piece of her insides kept dying and being shocked back to life over and over, and it wasn't entirely unpleasant.

He'd seemed unsure for parts of it. As always. Awkward and adorable. It was okay to think he was adorable because she was going to go on a date with him, so that was okay, right? But he only seemed unsure of whether or not she would say yes. All of her concerns, the things she'd agonized over, he'd blown past with easy, unblinking certainty. It blew her away.

He's sure he wants a date with me. What people might say—he didn't even care. He'd looked at her like those thoughts hadn't even occurred to him. Like they didn't matter to him nearly as much as she did.

She tried not to think about Mark. Tried so hard not to compare. It wouldn't be fair. Jay didn't even know about him. But everything with Mark had seemed so fresh. It was all just there. It had been so long since she felt like she mattered to someone that way, and even if it was just a first date and she was being goofy, she felt like she was melting. But not like the Wicked Witch melting. Like a peppermint stick in hot chocolate melting.

I might be in very big trouble here. Maybe the best kind of trouble. She'd never in her entire life been on a first date with someone she knew as well as she knew Jay. Someone she'd gotten to see when he was tired, when he was irritated, when he had messed up, when he was offended, when he was with people he knew well, and when he was with strangers. She realized her whole job experience in Silas Bend had allowed her an extensive interview of his character. She'd never in her entire life been on a first date with someone like Jay Marler.

"Shawley!" Piper didn't mean to shout as she entered through the front door sans shoes. But she also didn't quite stop shouting. "Jay asked me on a date!"

"I thought you and Jay were already dating."

Piper started at the unfamiliar voice and looked at the staircase where a curious and previously unknown middle-aged man with a Cheech Marin moustache was plodding slowly down.

"What?" she asked.

He shrugged and ambled past her on the way to the back patio. Sometimes she forgot that Shawley and Calvin did occasionally have other guests at their B&B.

Shawley appeared from the kitchen, looking overjoyed. Piper turned to her and pointed over her shoulder at the man heading out the door. "Shawley, do you and Calvin talk about your young friends like soap opera characters to guests?" By the time she'd finished her question, Shawley had one arm around her shoulders and had her squeezed into a lovely, comfortable side hug.

"Of course we do, Starlet. Only it's less like gossiping about soap stars and more like bragging about grandkids. Now you come in and tell me about this date."

Vaguely aware of the smile that took captive her entire face, possibly her entire being, Piper leaned into the warmth of her friend and told her, "He said he'd date me tonight if he could. So we're going on a date tonight 'cause we can."

Piper had had dinner with Jay dozens of times. Pizza in the office or snatched bites at events. Planning meetings at Olive's Café or something with Kent and Kariss. This wasn't the same as any of those times.

She found herself inexplicably nervous. Could a person have delayed whiplash? How had things with Jay just one-eightied? She'd been sure there would be nothing and then, boom, this unexpected something, and what even happened in between?

Furthermore, how did one date someone who was also friend and soon-to-be-former employer? They'd shared a million meals and good times, but none of them had been romantic. She'd never think of the word romantic the same way again. But the two of them had established patterns of behavior. Established patterns of behavior couldn't just be shifted. It wasn't like the movies where couples flirted and flirted and had these heavy, staring-deep-into-each-other's eyes, almost-kiss moments that led to romance. Piper and Jay didn't have that. She was pretty sure they'd never made eyes. Had they? She knew there were no almost-kisses.

So how did two people go from not-romance, not-romance, not-romance, to romance? What if she looked at him and tried to say something couple-y and ended up saying, "Hey, I have always admired your hair"? It was true, and it would be a stupid thing to say, and she was not prepared for this.

Except that she also wanted him to hurry and pick her up, and she wanted to see him, and what if he held her hand, because that was a thing people did on

248

dates—that would be all right, and normal people were probably not this obsessed about holding hands.

Shawley provided outfit counsel. Shawley was delighted to provide outfit counsel. Piper had to go digging in the storage area of the basement where they'd put the things she couldn't fit in her bedroom. There hadn't been a lot of need for snazzy outfits in Silas Bend, but Shawley assured her it wouldn't be weird to dress up a little for a date with Jay.

So she paid attention to her makeup and scrunched her hair. She had a lightweight lacy royal blue dress cut simply just above the knee with three-quarter sleeves and an empire waist. Casual enough she could wear it with sandals and wouldn't feel overdressed most places but still a far cry from her usual shorts and a t-shirt. Shawley said it looked darling, and darling was good. Calvin said she looked very pretty. The moustache man and his wife gave her a thumbs up. By then she was thoroughly done with curtseying.

She was waiting at the kitchen island when she heard him at the front door, and she stood to meet him in the foyer. The moment he saw her he stopped dead, and his mouth fell open. But it was his quiet, "Wow," that turned some of her awkward self-consciousness into delighted self-consciousness. Then she noticed he was in cargo shorts and the sneakers he used for hiking.

It occurred to her that they hadn't discussed what they'd be doing. "Oh. You're wearing…"

"Yes," he nodded without taking his eyes off her. "I thought we'd go hiking. I'm going to change all my plans."

"I can just go up and change real…"

"No," he said quickly. "No, you…" he trailed off with a little almost-laugh, and his face tinged pink. "Good grief, Piper," he said, quietly helpless, and he touched a hand to his temple before shaking his head, and he looked so taken she hardly knew what to do with herself. "You look beautiful."

A camera shutter sound effect graciously pulled Piper away from the moment enough to forestall any danger of her doing something really embarrassing like tearing up or hugging him or asking if she could touch his hair. Shawley stood with her phone, shamelessly taking pictures.

"Don't mind me." Shawley waved her hand at them. Then contradicted that by instructing, "Get closer together real quick."

"We're all aware this isn't prom?" Jay checked, but he acquiesced to standing awkwardly with her for the requisite awkward photos.

"Yes, yes." Shawley finished with her photography and shooed them off. "Go. Have fun."

Their first stop was Jay's little duplex where she waited for him to change into nice jeans and a button-up shirt. He said he knew a place in Northbury, 25 minutes away that would be fun. It occurred to her that she hadn't been outside the Silas Bend city limits in…possibly since she came to Silas Bend.

She sat in the passenger seat of Jay's car in her dress, and watched him tap the steering wheel the way he did. They'd had comfortable silences. This didn't feel like a comfortable silence. She'd wanted to be here, but now she was here, she didn't know how to be.

He didn't even look her way when he said, apropos of absolutely nothing, "When I first met you I nicknamed you 'Swampy' in my head. After a pregnant cat I had once."

"Wow," was all she could say.

"Just so we can establish that I'm obviously impaired and shouldn't be allowed to make decisions or influence people."

She laughed and he grinned, and the bubble of discomfort seemed to burst.

He tilted his head to glance over at her. "Do you want to hold hands with me?"

"Why yes. Yes, I do."

After that, she relaxed into the comfort of them that had already become familiar. Twenty-five minutes in the car went by the way time with him often did. With words and laughter and inconceivably quickly.

He'd picked a restaurant called The Theatre, a gorgeous old brick building with high ceilings, decorated with old-world charm and exposed brick and pipes. The signs boasted about their brick oven pizzas, and the brick oven itself looked suitably boast-worthy. Piper didn't realize until she got inside that half the place was a bowling alley, or indeed that a place with a bowling alley could still feel classy. But there were eight lanes and a counter to rent shoes. Low lighting and leather furniture scattered about added a certain intimacy, and the sounds of bowling pins somehow seemed farther away and less intrusive than it should.

They ordered a pizza to split and found a corner booth. While they waited, they talked about their friends. Jay told her he'd let Kent know about their date tonight, and he'd realized that was not something one should do the same way plugging a toaster in near the bathtub was not something one should do.

"Why would anyone need a toaster by the bathtub? Sick." She wrinkled her face. "Bath toast."

He stared at her. "You've ruined that metaphor for me forever. Like that was a go-to metaphor for me, and you've ruined it." Which led to an entire conversation about metaphors and idioms, and Jay confessed, "Any time I hear someone say 'So-and-so burst into tears,' I picture it literally. Every time."

"So you think of them just like…"

"Yes. Like a water balloon." He made a circle with his hands and mimed it blowing apart. "Pttsh."

"Gross."

"It's horrifying, I agree. And it's the worst thing because if somebody's being serious about it, telling me this story about somebody crying, I have to try really hard not to laugh."

"You monster."

His hands were warm and interesting, and occasionally he would reach across and brush his fingertips across the top of her hand for no reason she could fathom. It reminded her of the way he'd occasionally be restless or fidgety, except here he didn't look to be in any hurry to get up and do something. He looked happy. Happy to be there with her. To reach out and touch her hand because he could, and she felt so utterly conquered by her fondness for this man she would've been helpless in that moment to try to articulate it.

He prayed before they ate, and asked her about spiritual things, and she was amazed at how easy the conversation was. When he talked about the Lord, he was for real, and it reminded her of Colossians 3, the parts that said, "…Christ, who is your life…" and "…do everything in the name of the Lord Jesus…" Like Christ was Jay's life. His reason. And that made him more attractive even than the soft light that caught on the dark blues of his eyes and highlighted the fact that his eyelashes were the handsomest eyelashes a man could have. How had she never realized that, and what kind of a psycho found herself attracted to a man's eyelashes? Was there even a way to compliment a man's eyelashes that wouldn't come out sounding entirely strange?

After pizza they decided to bowl a lazy round. She got socks from a vending machine, and they rented shoes. Vending machine socks. That's right.

"Be honest," Piper said. "You brought me here because you want to see me do something clumsy with a bowling ball."

"You? Never."

"Good." She sniffed. "Because I'm not clumsy. If anything, I prefer the term 'ambisinister.'"

"That is not a word."

"It absolutely is."

They took their time and bowled, and Piper didn't do anything particularly ambisinister. She didn't hit an impressive amount of pins. But he didn't either, and it was all fine because she couldn't take bowling seriously, and he didn't seem to be too serious. She thought she should maybe tell him about Mark. About being engaged. About being so recently disengaged. But she couldn't force herself to do it—to inject that shot of inconvenient reality into what was otherwise in that moment beautifully ideal. Neither of them brought up her impending move either.

Jay drove her home, and the next thing she knew he was walking her up the porch steps to the front door of Shawley Bea's. He paused a moment, and she asked him if he wanted an iced tea or anything, which seemed odd because it wasn't her house and he could've gone in without knocking if he'd wanted. But he shook his head.

"So this...this was a good thing, yeah?" he asked.

"Yes. I believe so, yes. Definitely yes."

"So I remember saying I'd try not use the word romantic again."

"You've just broken your contract."

"Right. Well, good. Because you are now eligible for a... pretty romantic post-date kiss. Uh. Standard rates may apply. Should you like to opt out, please refer to the 'opt out' tab under Terms and Conditions, and..."

She leaned up and nearly missed his lips, but he was there, and she could feel his surprise and delight in the kiss. The hand that had held hers brushed along her cheek, brief, and then there was space between them again. But wow.

"Oh, thank you," he breathed. His happiness lit his face and warmed her to her toes. "I would've kept going with that ridiculous bit."

"It was a cute bit, though."

"It was going absolutely nowhere." He darted forward to peck her cheek in a move that was almost shy before he was pulling away, backing down the porch steps. "See you in the morning?"

"Yes, you will. Thanks for tonight."

He just grinned at her. A bright, boyish, beautiful thing, and Piper had to put her hand to her mouth to physically restrain a smile that would likely have been too much for her face to handle.

Calvin and Shawley were both in their chairs in the sitting room being conspicuous. "Well?" Shawley prompted.

Grateful for her practice at Kariss's days earlier, Piper put the back of her hand to her forehead and managed a proper graceful swoon onto the couch. Though this time, she had notably different reasons for being shamelessly melodramatic.

Jay filed his weekend under the header of "Best Couple Days in Personal Possibly Human History." It hardly felt like an exaggeration. He thought he'd been attached to Piper before. He'd been a foolish child then. Looking at her now was almost painful. In a wholly addictive way.

He sat next to her in church, and Jordan probably preached a fantastic sermon. Jay could not recall a word of it. He kept thinking about the previous evening and the girl sitting next to him tapping notes into her phone Bible while his mind carried him away to futures where he could sit next to her in every church service forever. He really ought to rein those sorts of thoughts in a little.

Sunday night he filled in for a friend who taught a small Bible study at her house. She'd gotten called out of town last minute and asked whether he'd want to take over for the night. Kent and Kariss volunteered their house, and when he asked Piper if she had any idea what he should talk about, she suggested Ruth.

The suggestion surprised him, but he studied Ruth that afternoon after lunch, and he found himself caught up in the story. At the Bible study, he talked about Naomi. About how, after she'd lost her husband and her sons and her home, she'd told people, "Do not call me Naomi," which means pleasant, "call me Mara," or bitter. And he talked about how, after Boaz married Naomi's daughter-in-law, Ruth, and Ruth gave birth to a child, the women said, "A son has been born to Naomi." She didn't argue her name then.

Mostly he talked about how sometimes it was human nature to cry abandonment and descend into bitterness when things hurt or there had been great loss. But all along, God was guiding Naomi, allowing her to have a hand in bringing Ruth and Boaz together. Not only had Naomi been redeemed, but she got to play a part in fulfilling God's plan to bring Jesus into the world. Despite her bitterness even.

He didn't say that sometimes, though he would've liked to be a Boaz coming to the rescue or a Ruth with unwavering loyalty and obedience, he felt more like a Naomi than anything. That instead of having the faith to search out God's purpose, he wanted to lean toward bitterness and self-pity and moving along at the speed of "me." It encouraged him that God still used Naomi, right where she was. That He flipped her life even when she didn't deserve it and proved Himself sovereign as He always was.

Jay liked teaching. He always felt like he learned more when he had to teach. The year before, he'd taught a Sunday school class at church, but it was ultimately too much on top of everything else. He'd ended up feeling unprepared more often than not. Maybe he should see if they had any classes that were still looking for a Sunday school teacher at the new school year. He should talk to Jordan about it.

He enjoyed talking to Jordan. The two didn't get to mix nearly as much as Jay would've liked. Jay stayed too busy, and he was sure Jordan had a million things to do, too. Running a community center likely had a few things in common with pastoring a church, logistics-wise and demanding-schedule-wise. Except that in addition to working with people in the realm of activities, Jordan had the task of leading and discipling them.

What if God wanted me to do that? The thought hit out of nowhere during the discussion, and Jay really needed to focus. Even so, he nearly snickered at the thought. He hadn't even managed to listen to a sermon that very morning. Seemed like that should be something of an indicator. Still, he'd always felt like he wanted to be involved in some type of ministry. What if God wanted him in, *ministry* ministry?

It was nonsense. He didn't have the schooling. Or the training. Or surely the whole host of other things he didn't even know pastors were supposed to have.

After the group closed with a prayer, most of the people hung around talking for awhile, but eventually the crowd dwindled to Jay, Piper, and the Peepers. Kariss had gone in to put JJ to bed, and Piper had disappeared into the kitchen. Kent sprawled on the couch next to Jay, a pillow over his face because he claimed Sundays made him sleepy.

"Hey," Jay said. "Do you think I'm good at teaching?"

"You taught me the value of friendship," Kent volunteered immediately without moving the pillow off his face. He held up a finger to add, "And how to use spreadsheets."

Jay nodded at that, even though his friend couldn't see him. *God, I'm probably too old to be wondering what I'm supposed to be when I grow up. But Lord, whatever You have for me, help me to have an attitude more like Ruth's and less like Naomi's. I trust You've got me figured out in ways that I don't. Just…whatever You'd have me do,*

258

whatever doors You want to open, Lord, push me through. I trust You.

CHAPTER TWENTY-THREE

Piper's last week at SBCC seemed like a curious combination of warm, sparkling, vigorous life and being gutted with the business end of a machete. She still avoided talking to Jay about leaving beyond the practical stuff of "This'll be my last workday," and "Emily's already picked up most of what I do, but you'll want to go over this and this with her."

He didn't talk about it much either, and they should. But she appreciated the silent agreement they'd made at some point to studiously ignore the 800 pound gorilla in the room. It was much more fun bantering back and forth about the seven-ounce stuffed monkey named Andrew that Kent let slip was Jay's best friend before Kent was. Upon her request, Jay had grudgingly dug Andrew out of storage to display in his office over his computer monitor.

Things didn't change much at work. They were too hectic to change much at work. Except occasionally

Jay would smile at her oddly or swipe at her bangs and say something like, "I really like you." And she could bump her shoulder against him when they walked or give him a quick hug and try not to say anything about his eyelashes.

Thankfully she didn't have to leave before her boys' summer basketball championship. Though she would definitely miss their end-of-basketball-season party the following week. She hated that. Saturday morning, it was difficult not to be somewhat melancholy, but Finn interviewed her in a very professional manner, and Arthur and the twins gave her hugs, and Noah burped the words, "Coach Piper," and it would have been impossible to not feel cheerier after that.

Hubcap G. Cope, dressed in SBCC blue and orange, made his usual mascotorial appearance. He looked about in his trademark unaffected manner, and the boys giggled at him and touched his shell and loved him like a puppy.

There were the moments when Dillon set a pick just the way they'd practiced and Chase nailed his layup when she was very proud of her team. And there were moments when Wayne double-dribbled and Kolby nearly ran the full length of the court in the wrong direction when she also was very proud of her team.

Overall, they finished third out of five, which seemed a heady victory. Each of the boys got a little bronze medal, and they jumped around and were loud little boys. Their parents thanked her and congratulated her and told her goodbye. At that point, reality took on some of the blurred, going-through-the-motions shades of disconnection. The way it tended to do at funerals.

She drove away from the gym afterwards with Hubcap in his box in the seat next to her, buckled in. "You have been an excellent companion on this adventure," she said to him. "If you were a frog and there was that precedent, I would kiss you."

He didn't seem disappointed. She found that reassuring.

Gravel crunched under her tires as she pulled off the road into the park, driving past campsites until she reached a secluded bend in the road and pulled her car off into the grass. She turned her car off and sat for a minute, surrounded by trees and wilderness. Remembered the first time she'd been stuck in a grove of trees with a turtle. "You turned out to be a wonderful detour, my friend. Worth the black eyes."

She picked Hubcap out of his carrier and went as far into the woods as she dared before she set him on a log like she'd found him.

It would be silly to get emotional. He was a turtle. Her pretend friend. He'd been a distraction and a toy, and she really, really, really liked him. Piper patted his shell, rubbed it with her thumb. Then she stood and went back to her car.

As she drove back to Shawley Bea's she felt a cry try to crawl up her throat, no doubt a long, ugly, unstoppable cry that would likely end in a headache. She pursed her lips and breathed through her nose and did not grant it passage. It was close, though.

Unexpectedly, Jay waited on the porch at Shawley Bea's. He stood as she got out of the car. "Hey.

I heard the Terror-pins got third. Wanna celebrate?" He trailed off when his eyes fell on Hubcap's empty carrier. His expression changed into something much more commiserating.

Piper cleared her throat and spoke tentatively in case her voice didn't come out sounding as strong as she preferred. "Laurel and her husband's apartment is No Pets. So. Just did, you know. A Free Willy sort of thing."

"He leaped over you to freedom in the open ocean?" Jay kidded gently. Then he took Hubcap's box in one hand and gathered her into a hug with the other. It was annoyingly sentimental while she was trying very hard not to be sentimental. But also, he felt wonderfully real and solid and comforting, and she didn't struggle at all not to lean into him.

"He was the greatest turtle to ever live," she said into his chest.

"I agree."

"He couldn't have been any greater if he was mutant and a ninja."

His mouth was against her temple. "Of course not. And he was remarkably mature."

"He was. Yes."

"He's still alive," he said kindly.

Piper sighed. "I know."

"Hey, I was thinking. What if you didn't leave?"

"Jay," she huffed a tired laugh and pulled away. "Have you ever heard of a smooth segue?"

"I'm not completely joking," he said as he let her go. He glanced down and stuck his hands in his pockets. "I'm not actually joking. At all. Is that… Is that even an okay thing to not be joking about? Because I've been thinking…"

"I can't."

"Hear me out, though."

"But I can't. I have a job lined up there. And even if I didn't, I can't keep staying here. Shawley and Calvin aren't making a dime on me. They're the best, most gracious people in the world, and I can't keep taking advantage of them. And my job belongs to Emily now. We don't have the budget for three of us full time. I can't just come back. I wouldn't do that to her."

"We could figure it out. There are other places you could work."

Piper shook her head. "I've done this before. Jumped in without looking. Moved across the country for a guy. It was a bad choice." She saw the spark of something cross his face and realized she had to tell him, "I was engaged to be married up until about three weeks before I met you."

Was that even possible? It felt like a hundred years ago when it didn't feel like yesterday. "Which I should have told you. I…you definitely should have been made aware of that before right now. But it was a mess. And this…this isn't the same as that, I understand that." She sounded defensive to her own ears, and that wasn't how she wanted to sound.

264

Piper consciously relaxed and made the effort to look him in the eye. "Look, I like you. A lot. An unbelievable lot. And I want you-and-me to work. So much. But there is no way I can justify cobbling my life together around you after one date. And there's no way you should try to cobble your life together around me. I mean I can't speak for you, but I know I'm not in any place to make that kind of decision right now. It wouldn't be wise. I have family and a job waiting for me, and I don't get to tell them to just wait."

Looking him in the eye was difficult. She liked his eyes. She liked lots of things about him, and the past week of jokes and banter and bright conversation had been so much better than everything this was. "Thank you for wanting me to stay," she said quietly. "But please don't ask me to."

Jay stood watching her for a long few moments, his hands still in his pockets. Looking her in the face and thinking, and sometimes she thought they must share a brain, but this wasn't one of those times. She prepared herself for questions and arguments and *Engaged?* "Okay," he said finally. Then he quirked his lips in a painful smile. "This isn't fun."

Grateful, she shook her head, "No."

"Ice cream is fun," he mused.

"It is."

"Ice cream with you. That is a party."

She still had packing to do. There was a zero percent chance that would take precedence. "Want to hold hands with me?" she asked, the way he had the week before.

"Why, yes." He reached out his hand to her. "All the time."

It had been two weeks. The day after she left, Piper had e-mailed him a color-coded schedule chart with optimum times for phone or video chat highlighted. It didn't really help much with their ability to communicate. But he thought it probably helped her to make it. He'd printed it regardless and given it to Andrew to hold in his monkey hands with the aid of a couple of safety pins. Because if Andrew was going to live in his office, he should make himself useful.

It was just after ten in the evening, and Jay was alone in the community center. He stretched out on his green couch under the picture Piper gave him and pressed her name on his phone screen. He slipped his free hand under his head and tried to remember details of how she'd looked the day he met her as he waited for her voice.

"Hello?" Piper answered.

He felt himself relax. "Hello."

"Does it seem a little inauthentic to use the word 'hello' over the phone? Since I don't think I ever say 'hello' in non-electronically mediated conversations."

"You do sometimes."

"I do?"

"Yeah. But you usually say it ironically."

"Oh." He pictured the way she twisted her mouth sometimes when she was thinking and wished he could see it. Talking on the phone with her was fun, but it was also a little like having lots of blood drawn. "Well then I'll keep saying hello when I answer the phone."

"Good." He took his hand back from behind his head and tapped his fingers on his chest. "Tell me your thoughts on flowers."

"God made them!" she said brightly. Then her voice became immediately analytical. "But I do think they're overrepresented in almost all forms of art."

Jay blinked and scratched the back of his head. "I was actually wondering if you had a favorite kind, but your response was remarkable." He didn't get to hear her reply because of the booping sound in his ear. He glanced at it, didn't recognize the number. "Hey, babe? I'm getting another call. Can I call you right back?"

"Sure."

Jay sat up and switched the call over. "Hello?" And for a moment, all he could think about was whether he used "hello" in normal conversations.

"Jay Marler? Hi, this is Daniel Barber. You remember I worked with you for a few months, oh, two years ago now, I guess?"

"Daniel. Hey, man, yeah." They'd done a summer together at SBCC. It took a second to pull together a composite. He remembered a tall guy in his late twenties. Dark hair and freckles and shy if he remembered right. Great worker, and they'd gotten along really well. "How are you?"

"Doing fine. Sorry to call so late, but I had kind of a random question for you."

"Shoot."

"Well, I'm at Northbury Community Church. It's pretty tiny, about 200 on a Sunday. You might not know it."

"No, I know it. Sure." Jay stood and went to his desk to find a pen, assuming Daniel wanted to schedule an event or something.

"Okay, well, we've been without a pastor for about six months, and I'm one of the people on the search committee. So we've been searching and praying. It's been slow, but we've seen a couple people we're kind of interested in. Then last week I think it was, you popped into my head. I was remembering working with you, and then I started thinking about you and the stuff you're doing in Silas Bend. Honestly, I know this is out of the blue, but I feel like God wouldn't leave me alone about it. But are you...would you be at all interested in applying for a pastorate in Northbury? Would that make any sense to you at all?"

Jay could only, ineloquently, "Uh…"

"This isn't even a job offer. It's not how we do things. I haven't talked to the rest of the committee or anyone really about it. I'm assuming you're still really involved running SBCC. But I just couldn't get your name out of my head. So you feel free to shoot me down right here. But if you wanted to pray about it…"

"I could…yeah, I could pray about it. Should I send you a resume, or…? I mean I'm not qualified. It'll say I'm not qualified. I don't have the education. I've got a…an associates in business."

"Yeah, send it. We can talk more. Nothing's set in stone. Nothing's set in…paper-mâché at this point. I just honestly didn't even think you would be interested. Felt like I was losing my mind."

"You might be losing your mind. But I am interested."

Daniel gave him his e-mail address and promised to call later in the week so they could meet up and talk. After ending the call, Jay swiveled his head to check that everything in the office was still the same. *Did I just get sucked into another dimension?* He hit Piper's number again.

"Hello," she answered very deliberately.

"Hi. I just got the most bizarre phone call of my life."

Emotionally, Piper thought she was doing pretty well, all things considered. Her job was the soul-sucking drudgery of muted colors and dark slacks and talking

269

on the phone to people who didn't want to talk to her. But she'd gotten a mid shift, 1-9 instead of overnights, so that was a huge plus. And anyway, jobs were supposed to involve some level of soul-sucking drudgery. She'd expected that going in. Although if it started turning her into whatever sort of insentient wraith stole her sandwich out of the fridge on Tuesday, she was out of there.

Kariss helped. Semi-frequent, contextless texts and the occasional artsy photograph featuring JJ's soulful face.

Laurel and her husband Matt were great to give up the office in their apartment for Piper's use. The walls were a bright, sunny yellow. She had a daybed and a desk that could function as a dresser, and everything was clean and nice and perfectly satisfactory.

Even if life seemed all at once still.

Piper and Laurel were so polite to each other. Polite the way no sisters should ever have to be. Piper knew how to fix it, but she kept chickening out. She didn't know how to apologize without opening an entire volcano's worth of stuff and spewing it all over Laurel. Which seemed rude. And terrible. And inevitable.

Everything was perfectly satisfactory even if she thought about Kariss and Kent and JJ and Shawley and Calvin and SBCC and yearned. And even if she heard Jay's voice or got a text and wanted so much to be there instead of here.

Except her prayers lately were mostly about, *Lord, give me the courage and wisdom to make here good. And*

Father, I believe You and trust You to lead me. Please give me an attitude of peace and contentment. And sometimes just, Jesus, my heart aches.

Overall, though, she thought she'd been pretty solid emotionally. But then at ten in the morning in her borrowed office-room, she noticed a notification on her phone and found a link sent to her by Tony Jasper, the father of the basketball twins. When she clicked, it led to a private video.

Curious, she tucked her feet under her on the day bed as the video started to play. It began with a dramatic drumbeat before an animated logo for "The Silas Bend Terrapins!" burst into view. Piper found herself laughing out loud as it faded into a clip of an early scrimmage where none of them, least of all her, knew what they were doing.

The video had some very sophisticated transitions. They came between images of her explaining the lifecycle of a moth to Dillon for reasons she couldn't remember and the tall brunette nodding with the sort of baffled resignation that would serve him well in all his relationships. Noah's thundercloud brows undermined by an almost-smile as she poked his cheek. Chase lying flat on his back in the middle of the floor during one practice proclaiming, "Coach! I am fresh out of basketball!" She remembered that had led to the rest of her team dropping to the floor, giggling for ten minutes.

Finn added a dramatic voice-over that delivered a not-entirely-accurate account of their journey from league underdogs to league champions—in spite of the fact they had come in third.

Jay's face showed up, too. In one instance she didn't even remember, he lobbed a shot from half court that missed wildly, bounced off the wall and nailed Arthur in the back of the head. Which might not have been as funny as it was had Finn not captured the gasping look of horror on Jay's face.

The video ran over twelve minutes, and Piper couldn't say for sure at what point she started crying. Sometime before the gag real started, she knew that. The tears wouldn't be stopped, and she had expected them. She'd been swallowing around cry-throat for weeks now. Still, she found herself indignant about the first real sob that broke from her chest. The tears were inconvenient as, in addition to being unattractive, they made viewing a video difficult.

By the time the video cut to black and the music faded out, Piper tilted sideways onto her pillows and let herself cry. She didn't have anywhere to be until one o'clock. Plenty of time. A good, rejuvenating cry. If she thought about the tears falling from her eyes and snot dripping from her nose and chest constricting around each sobbing breath as though it were all a kind of spa treatment, it seemed much more pleasant. And had the added benefit of keeping her mind off all the reasons why she was crying.

A sudden light tap at the door startled Piper, and she sat up to see Laurel looking uncomfortable and sympathetic in the doorway. "Is this an alone kind of cry, or...?"

Piper sniffed and moved over, waving with her phone as she wiped her face with her other hand. "Watch this with me."

Laurel came in and sat next to her. It took almost the whole twelve-plus minute video for Piper to get a hold of herself.

"You coached basketball," Laurel said as it ended. "It's good you have video evidence."

"The kid who made this video is only eleven." He was also her spirit animal.

"That's impressive."

"I want to adopt him and raise him and tell everyone I'm responsible for how awesome he is."

Laurel nodded and sat quietly for a moment. Her light brown hair was straightened and pulled away from her face with a headband. Her makeup was understated, her face lovely, the way all of Laurel was. She had great eyebrows. Like really phenomenal, well-shaped eyebrows. She looked so together, and Piper felt like the perfect contrast for all of that.

"Was Jay in there anywhere?" Laurel asked. She knew Piper talked to a guy named Jay.

Piper wouldn't have thought her sister would've understood enough to ask about him. "Mmhm. The panicky looking guy who hit the kid with a basketball."

Laurel grinned. "Ah, of course. He's cute." She looked at Piper, furrowing her perfect eyebrows in question. "You don't really talk about him," she said. "But I guess we haven't really been talking. Much. If you want to, though. I promise I won't say anything about him."

Piper nearly started crying again. She didn't. Definitely a crying near miss. Laurel shouldn't feel the need to be gentle to Piper. Shouldn't have to tread on the eggshells Piper had left in the wake of her mess-making.

"You were right about Mark," she said. It was difficult. Not because it wasn't true. It was inescapably true. And not because of her pride. She'd had her pride crushed and repackaged and handed back to her enough times in the past few months to make that a non-issue. It was difficult because Piper felt terrible about how she'd been. It hurt to look at her sister and confront her own failure and the consequences of that failure. Tears pricked her eyes, and her face kept trying to screw itself into uncomfortable shapes.

Laurel winced. Then appeared as though she hadn't meant to wince. "I didn't need you to say it."

"I needed me to say it. To you. Would've been nice if I could've said it two years ago."

Piper had thought herself so unfairly judged. Laurel had told her, "Hey, I don't think he gets you, Piper. You should be with someone who gets you. I don't like how he talks to you sometimes."

274

Piper had gone straight into defense mode. Defended him. Defended her choice. Because who was Laurel to tell her she was wrong? Laurel with her four years' extra life experience and her perfect husband and her arched eyebrows? It had been easier in the end to cut Laurel out and move forward with the life she was designing for herself. "I should've come to you a long time ago and said it. You shouldn't have had to initiate this conversation. I was wrong. You were right."

Laurel pressed her lips together. Piper knew her sister didn't like these sorts of conversations any more than she did.

"I didn't like being right about Mark," Laurel assured.

"Clearly I didn't like you being right about Mark either. I acted like an idiot. I was a grade A jerk to you. And I was so...righteous about it. I'm sorry. I'm very, very sorry, Laurel."

"I'm sorry, too. I didn't handle any of it like I should have."

Piper recognized that as a sympathy reciprocal apology.

She must have made a face because Laurel went on, "No, really. I could've been more mature. I was mad at you. I got my feelings hurt and I threw up my hands. For a long time."

Piper shrugged. "If I'd thrown up my hands about Mark when you did, I might have protected us both from the inevitable explosion. So."

Laurel leaned forward and hugged her. Laurel always hugged too tight, and with the expected huff of air leaving her lungs, Piper let out a little laugh that seemed to carry a lot of her stored-up tension with it.

"I am very sorry," Piper said again. She found the words easier to say while being hugged. She didn't understand the science of that, but she was grateful for it.

"Shut up now," Laurel commanded sweetly.

Piper dropped her head onto her sister's shoulder.

When they pulled back, Laurel confided, "I'm kinda glad you're here."

"Me, too."

"Mm. But you're kinda not glad you're here." Laurel said with older-sister authority, "You need to tell me about your summer."

"I befriended a turtle who started out as my mortal enemy. And I fell in love with the man who supplied my armor." She said the last to sound suitably dramatic. But she felt her face grow warm when she said it and hoped her leftover cry-blotchiness covered for her.

"I'm going to make popcorn," Laurel said immediately and scrambled up.

"Yes."

CHAPTER TWENTY-FOUR

It was a rare event for Jordan and his family, Jay, and the Peepers to all make it to Shawley and Calvin's for Sunday dinner. It was definitely the first time Jay had called each of them specifically to ask that they please come because he had something he wanted to discuss with them. After a meal of sandwiches and potato salad, the adults stayed seated around the table while Jordan's two little girls and JJ ran out to the backyard with watermelon slices that would no doubt leave them absolutely wrecked by the time their parents were ready to go.

Jay hadn't decided how best to broach the subject when Kent leaned back with his arm around his wife's chair and said, "So dude. Why'd you gather your brain trust?"

Segues didn't come any smoother than that.

Jay told them about Daniel's phone call and about the lunch they'd shared Wednesday afternoon. Jay had pointed out the millions of things that should have discouraged Northbury Community Church from wanting him to pastor. Daniel hadn't flinched. They'd prayed together for awhile, asking for guidance and discernment, and Daniel left excited. The man was excited about presenting Jay to his committee. Daniel wanted to move forward. They scheduled a phone meeting about the Northbury interview process for Monday morning.

Jay explained to them about how it would obviously mean stepping down from his position at Silas Bend Community Center.

At that point Jordan's little towheaded six-year-old came running in to tattle that "JJ is too high in the tree!"

Kent scraped his chair back and stood. They were all used to him having to go have a talk about physics and gravity with his four-year-old child. "He's going to be a stunt man by the time he's nine. Just watch."

As Kent left, Jay turned to the rest of them. "So. I guess I just wanted to ask you to pray and to see what you thought. About all of it."

"I think the timing is pretty impeccable," Calvin said with an air of satisfaction.

"Yeah. I mean, it seems ideal. But I'm still torn. Even at its most...headache-inducing, SBCC's been home. It's where I grew up. It's where I feel most comfortable. And it's my dad's. Part of me thinks there would be something dishonoring in that. And I don't doubt God put me there."

"Well, baby, God puts us lots of places," Shawley said. "That doesn't mean we have to stay there forever. Life comes in seasons. All of life. And I knew your daddy. Sweetheart, he started the community center because he wanted to serve God where he was. He wanted to be obedient. Just like you want to be. There isn't any way he could feel dishonored by a son who wants the same thing."

"She's right." Calvin nodded. "She's absolutely right."

"You know," Jordan said, "God gives us choices, too. When Adam and Eve were in the garden, God didn't say 'You can only eat from this one tree.' He told them they could eat from any tree except the one. If they ate from that one, that would be sin. But the rest were there for them to choose, for them to enjoy. I think sometimes we agonize over these decisions, about which one thing God has for us when He's given us choices. You do a great job at the community center. But if you've prayed about this pastorate opportunity and you think it's something you would enjoy and something you'd be effective at, I'd tell you not to hold back."

Jay let his words—God's words—soak in.

"I think when you make a decision like this," Jordan said, "caution is definitely warranted and wise. But I've seen how your heart works, and I know how you love the Lord. So even if you're not immediately successful or it doesn't work out like you'd like, I don't think you need to be afraid of disappointing God. Or of somehow moving outside of His plan for your life."

Jay raised his eyebrows as he nodded. "I hadn't thought of that. Yeah."

Jordan quirked a smile and finger-gunned a thank you. "I use the same analogy when I talk dating with the teenagers."

"Awesome."

"And I have to say, too," Jordan went on, "that if God really is calling you to pastor, He's not going to leave you alone about it—whether this church works out or not. If He decides to close this door? Then you need to seek out the next pastor-type door."

Jay nodded slowly.

"Have you talked to Piper about it?" Kariss asked, and Jay couldn't understand the nature of her grin.

"A little bit, yeah."

The nature of her grin seemed scarily omniscient. "Good."

Before he could ask what that meant, Kent walked back in with a sulky, chastised-looking little boy beside him. JJ stepped away from his dad and reached for Jay in a clear display of spite, but Jay picked him up anyway and let him hide his hot, slightly teary face in Jay's neck while grumbling specifically and unintelligibly about the unfairness of life.

"What'd we miss?" Kent asked. "We still talking about Jay being a pastor at Northbury?"

"Yes. I need your two cents."

"I have a ton of sense. Dude. You'd make an epic pastor. Anyway, don't you do a lot of the pastoring stuff already? Like you listen to people and counsel folks and pray for them and visit them when you can and love on difficult people and generally do all the leadership stuff."

"Thanks." Could it be that God had been using all his years at SBCC to prepare him for his next season? His next ministry? "I haven't done a lot of the preaching side, though," he said, not willing to let the point go completely.

"Psh. What about all the Bible studies and Sunday school classes you've taught? Total prep-work. And besides, even if you don't think you're there, you'll get it with practice. I mean I don't know, but...seems like it'd be a lot easier to teach a bro how to preach than to teach a bro how to pastor."

Silence from around the table as Jay digested that. "You're kind of profound sometimes."

Kent's raised eyebrow was more pointed than a ninja star. "Sometimes?"

The October air tasted crisp and smelled like burning leaves as Piper poured herself out of the backseat of Matt and Laurel's gray Cavalier onto the driveway of one of her favorite places in the entire world. Shawley

Bea's appeared even more splendid nestled into the backdrop colors of autumn leaves. Silas Bend in sweater weather beat Silas Bend in summer by a number of marks, and Piper hadn't thought that could be done.

"Holy smacks, this place is cute," Laurel declared as she closed the passenger door.

"See? I told you," Piper said. "This is why you had to come visit."

"Mm," Laurel agreed. "I want to live here forever. Matt, let's live here forever."

Matt had recently turned 30 and in his maturity had become inexhaustibly longsuffering. He nudged his glasses up with his shoulder as he took their bags out of the trunk. "Let's start with the weekend?" he suggested.

"I don't think my feelings will change," Laurel said. "Moving our wardrobe is going to be a nightmare."

Fortunately he'd been longsuffering even before he'd turned 30 because it was a quality that served him well in his relationship with Laurel. Piper recognized it as a quality her own man required much of. Who were these poor saps who willingly subjected themselves to prolonged periods of time with either of them?

"Hey!" Speaking of, Jay appeared at the front door of Shawley's and hopped off the porch without bothering with steps.

"Favorite!" she called happily. Next she knew, she was swept up in a hug that contained weeks of missing and longing and wishing, and he was dropping kisses on her face.

"You," he said, between kisses, "Are. So. Important."

He still made her melt. It was embarrassing. He didn't even have to try. She squeezed him around his middle. "Never don't be hugging me."

Jay laughed. She liked his laugh so much. "What?"

"Jay hugs are best hugs." She could no longer contain the words, "I missed you."

No natural or synthetic material existed that could shield her from the intensity of his smile in that moment.

"Hi, Starlet! Oh, you're here!"

Piper reluctantly pulled away from Best Hug, to turn toward Shawley. "Shawley Bea!" she called. She linked her fingers with Jay's and turned to Laurel and Matt. "Come on, I'll introduce you to everybody. Are Kent and Kariss here?"

"Yep, and they brought JJ," Jay answered.

Piper pulled and herded everybody up onto the porch where Calvin had joined his wife, and the Peepers were pushing their way out behind him.

"Piperrrrrrr!" Kent hollered. "And her familyyyyyy!"

Piper hugged everyone and laughed and introduced Laurel and Matt. There was such a feeling of home she was nearly delirious with it. Kariss gave her a brief, hard hug. Brief as it was, in those few moments,

Kent managed to relate to her everything his family had done in the two months since she'd left—even though she'd snatched a couple weekend visits solo since then.

She was honored when JJ, after some contemplation, deigned to perch on her shoulders. Like if a boy could be a cat could be a falcon. She relayed that thought to Kariss who seemed enamored of it and appeared to be considering some boy/cat/falcon fusion sculpture or something that would be creepy and amazing.

"Well hey, we should take our stuff inside," Piper said.

"Hang on." Jay repossessed JJ and handed him to his mother, then took Piper's hand and pulled her further down the porch as if it offered greater privacy.

Which was laughable as Piper immediately felt everyone's eyes on them.

"I have something to tell you." Jay's voice had gone low and quiet, but he was all but vibrating with excitement.

She couldn't think of a time he looked more attractive. She leaned forward. "Like a secret?" Piper had a feeling she knew. The interviews had seemed to go on forever, but he had to have heard something by now.

Jay grinned. "Like not a secret." He let go of her hand and took hold of her shoulders as if to physically ground her in preparation for hearing his not-a-secret. "The committee voted for me," he said. "Babe, I'm preaching in front of the church on Sunday, and the church members are going to vote. If they vote me in, I'm going to get to start as soon as I can."

"You are kidding me!" His hands on her shoulders did nothing to prevent her jumping into the air where she was. She threw her arms around his neck. Piper could hardly believe it. This could be real. This looked like a real thing that was happening, and bizarrely, she wanted to cry, but she was laughing. "I knew it, though! I mean, I didn't. Ugh, that's so awesome!" She pushed away, and this time it was her hands on his shoulders. "Praise God." *Praise my wonderful, amazing, perfect, omnipotent God. Lord, are You showing off? What are You trying to do to me?*

She saw her man beaming.

"The church is going to pay for me to take online seminary classes *while I work there*. I'm going to be taking Bible classes while I work there."

"Get out of here. That's amazing!" She looked around Jay to the Silas Benders—Silas Benders, she should remember that for later—and pointed a gleefully accusing finger. "You people! Did you know this news?"

Kent shouted back, "Yes! I super almost told you in the ten minutes since you got here, but I didn't!"

Jay turned Piper back to face him. "So. God-willing, this happens. Let's talk logistics."

"I love logistics so much," Piper said seriously.

"I know you do. Now I am going to need someone to take over at SBCC. So I was thinking… Someone who is a thousand times more organized than me. Has on-the-job experience. Is almost offensively likeable. Has brown eyes and a pretty face."

She found herself floundering less than halfway through his speech. "It can't be the Jaspers' golden retriever."

"I'm serious."

"I know!" She could come back. She could run SBCC. She could live here. All the time. "We didn't even talk about... I can't...I am processing what you're saying, and there is an unknown error..."

"Do you want to?"

And she found that, "Yes! Wait. Yes! I want to. I can't even handle how much I want to. But Jay...I mean... When? What... I'm going to have to move. I would need a place to stay..."

"Oh, you can stay here, of course," Shawley called from the doorway. She had the grace not to bother pretending she hadn't been eavesdropping. She winked. "At least til the wedding." The woman looked around and shrugged without apology. "We're all thinking it."

Kent giggled, slung an enthusiastic arm around the woman and kissed her cheek. "I love you so much, Ms. Shawley."

She patted his face affectionately. "I love you, too, darling."

Piper might have been nodding or she might have been shaking her head. "This is so much. So much, so much."

"Good?" Jay asked, and there was no way he didn't already know the answer to that question.

"Unbelievable. Jay, it's unbelievable."

"I got you a present." He looked terribly proud of himself as he pulled a long, rectangular cardboard box from his jeans pocket.

"You got me a present," she said with the aww very much implied as she took it from him. She pulled the top off the box and found a small, oval-shaped locket. Pretty silver and etched with an ivy design. Piper glanced up at his face and only sounded a little teasing when she told him, "This is super romantic."

"Open it."

Piper handed him the box and worked the locket open. She expected pictures of the two of them. She found two tiny pictures of the handsomest, most masculine, most fantastic turtle to ever step in front of a car and become her friend. It was so unexpected she froze for a moment. "This is a million times more romantic than I even imagined." He laughed at her. How close had she come to never getting to hear that laugh?

Piper turned around so he could do the necklace clasp behind her neck. It touched her, probably more than Jay intended. Because what had God done? In the middle of her wrecked life, God had sent exactly the roadblock she needed. When she had no idea she needed it. She remembered that road and the rain and her life and the turtle. She remembered feeling in every sense derailed. But somehow that had led to this.

Father, You are incredible. I always want to praise You. God, I don't even have the words now. Hear my heart, Lord, because it is full, overflowing with love for You. Lord, help me remember this moment. This feeling. These praises. Because You have blessed me more than I ever could have seen coming, and I want to remember exactly this on the days life seems too hard. On the days when there are too many roadblocks and detours, I want to remember how you use the terrible and the terrapins to work in the lives of Your people. Glory to You, Jesus. Glory, glory, glory.

"Piper, what are you doing?" Jay's voice by her ear interrupted her, and she realized she'd closed her eyes.

"I am babbling a thanksgiving prayer like a lovesick fool," she said without opening them.

"Oh." He sounded amused. "Well, go ahead."

"No, it's fine. It's ongoing," she said, drawing a deep breath before opening her eyes and turning to face him.

His hand found hers as they turned back to face their rather happy, happy family. They all stood in the fading light of an October sunset together, blatantly watching Piper and Jay. Except for Kent who was chattering happily at Matt about...some kind of saw?

"I do want to have a wedding," Jay murmured out the side of his mouth. "With you, I mean. Like Shawley said. I have intentions. I mean this isn't me asking, obviously. Just I obviously love you and will ask you for a wedding. I mean to marry me." He shook his head with a bewildered expression.

The warmth in her chest could've heated the entire continent. "I hope it goes just like that." Very quietly, she thought, *Oh. I'm going to be a pastor's wife.* It was another unexpected blessing she couldn't have written for herself. That God would even use all her mistakes, all her wrongly-reasoned research to prepare her for a new journey. How humbling. Because now, much more loudly, much more importantly, I'm going to be Jay Marler's wife.

Jay smiled a slightly self-conscious smile. "Babe, this is going to be all new for me. Most of …everything. I don't have everything figured out yet."

"Me neither."

"And you're good with that?" he checked, a faint line of nervousness running between his eyebrows.

She looked straight into his eyes and told him from the core of her being, "I am so good with that."

ACKNOWLEDGMENTS

Without Richie Rhea, Kaley Faith Rhea simply wouldn't be here. And Rhonda Rhea would certainly feel altogether unfinished. Huge thanks to the best dad/husband ever created.

Additional enthusiastic nods of thanks to amazing family members for the best ever cheerleading and all kinds of ministry support. We love you, Andy Rhea, Amber Rhea, Jordan Rhea, Allie Rhea McMullin, Derek McMullin, Daniel Rhea and Olivia Rhea. Asa Rhea and Emerson McMullin also get nods of thanks for inspiring us with their intense cuteness—and for increasing the family's overall cuteness factor in a way that only the world's cutest babies could.

Much gratitude as well to Rhonda's prayer team: Janet Bridgeforth, Tina Byus, Diane Campbell, Mary Clark, Theresa Easterday, Chris Hendrickson, Melinda Massey and Peanuts Rudolph. We simply can't overvalue the investment made on the knees of these godly women.

A huge shout-out of thanks to our amazing agent, Pamela Harty, and to all those at the Knight Agency who help make it possible for us to do what we love to do.

Thankful hugs to the ever-likeable, all-around great folks, George and Karen Porter, and to all the folks at Bold Vision Books, especially Amy Allen. We love working with a publishing house that understands heart ministry and that makes us feel more like family than colleagues.

Cynthia Ruchti. Oh, Cynthia Ruchti. Editor and book counselor, extraordinaire. Your skill, wisdom and sharp eye made this book so much better. Your personality and ardent wit made the process way more fun. How can we ever thank you?

Special thanks to Steve and Betty Rhoads for helping us work out details for a week of manic writing. We feel we owe you a week of our lives. Each of us. So two weeks altogether. I have no idea how you'll collect, but we're sending along our sincere gratitude in the meantime.

Huge appreciation to the Advanced Writers and Speakers Association and to American Christian Fiction Writers. We so appreciate shared knowledge, prayers, support, encouragement, and counsel.

A personal nod of acknowledgment and thanks from Kaley to Katherine Burt, Hannibal LaGrange University's former English Department Chair, who always made English classy. Thank you for sweet talks in the office when it was supposed to be work time. Much gratitude for all the great inspiration and advice and for such amazing pleasantness. What a great lady.

We're both also so very thankful for Christian Television Network's KNLJ in Jefferson City, Missouri. Station Manager and sweet girlfriend, Vickie Davenport—what would we do without your encouragement and support and your amazing ministry helps?

And to those who labor alongside Rhonda at *HomeLife* magazine, *Leading Hearts* magazine, Edie Melson's *The Write Conversation, MTL* magazine, *The Pathway*, the Missouri Baptist Convention's official news journal, and other print and online publications who graciously grant space for Rhonda's humor columns, thank you.

And more head-bobs of thanks to our church families at Troy First Baptist Church and Northroad Community Church for consistent prayers and encouragement.

Our biggest and most straight-from-the-heart gratitude is reserved to the One who changed our lives for eternity through the redemptive work on the cross, and who grants grace for every bump in every road. How blessed we are to be His!

ABOUT THE AUTHORS

Mother/daughter writing duo, Rhonda Rhea and Kaley Rhea, are TV personalities for Christian Television Network's KNLJ. Rhonda is also a nationally-known speaker, humor columnist and author of 11 other books, including *Fix-Her-Upper*, a soon-releasing nonfiction project coauthored with Beth Duewel. Rhonda is married to her pastor/husband, Richie Rhea, and they have five grown children. Kaley and Rhonda both live in the St. Louis area.

MORE BOOKS FROM BOLD VISION BOOKS

Romantic Mystery from
LISA WESSEL

Could grief and devastation be imprinted on DNA and passed down through generations? Sophie Cahill believes it's the reason for her cautious heart.

A savage attack and sabotage endanger her plans for Covenant Falls' First Annual Founders Day. Will her dream job be the only thing she loses?

From Authors
Beth Duewell and Rhonda Rhea

Learn to develop hope and laughter through a God-renovated life.

CPSIA information can be obtained
at www.ICGtesting.com
Printed in the USA
LVHW04s1235091018
592959LV00004B/380/P

9 781946 708038